you so much. I hope you enjoy the book. Dive love, Jwod

S.E.X.

...She is a force to be reckoned with...

ISBN 9798656266864

For more information on the content of this book, email authortracywashington@gmail.com

JMPinckney Publishing Company, LLC,

Sonja Pinckney Rhodes, South Carolina

Illustration and Design: Michael Jooce Warren

Printed in the United States of America

A Novel

by

Dr. Tracy L. Washington

DEDICATION

This book is dedicated to my entire support system (family, friends, friends of friends, and sorors.) To avoid omitting my appreciation to everyone, I decided to make my life and yours easy:

(insert your name here), thank you for helping me in yet another memorable moment, I have accomplished in this amazing, yet crazy life of mine. You have been such a big help with (insert your action here) and I appreciate you for being the person that you are in my life. I would not be who I am if you did not have my back.

Love you much,

Dr. T.W.

The names, identity, and locations have been changed to protect the innocent and **definitely** the guilty.

Prologue

"You Bitch! I'm going to kill you!" She screamed.

She grabs me by my hair, and we both fall to the floor. During the struggle, I get the upper hand...so I thought.

"Slaaaap!"

The strange woman slaps me so hard, I momentarily blacked out. When I regained consciousness, I see double. There she is with a gun in my face.

"What do you have to say for yourself, hoe?"

I asked her, "Who are you? What do you want? Why are you here?"

I have no clue who she is, how she got in my house, and, more importantly, what in the hell does she want.

She waves the gun at me as she screams on the phone to someone.

"How could you let this happen? What did I do wrong? What do you see in this bitch?"

Now, I'm pissed! I feel blood drip down from my face; my $300 Donna Karan dress is now worth about $3.00, and this deranged bitch has the nerve to be upset... Really? Who does this?

She hangs up the phone and focuses her attention back to me, then asks the million-dollar question. "Why are you fucking my man?"

The question I am asking myself is…

Who in the hell is her man?

Stephanie (S.E.X.)

Stephanie Elizabeth Xavier (S.E.X.) is a 28-year-old honor graduate from Hampton University. As number one in her class, she reigned supreme as summa cum laude. Stephanie has a drive and desire unparalleled by her peers. Her laser focus led her to the field of finance. She's a successful Finance Director at William & Wilson Law Firm. Although she works hard in her field, there are whispers about her quick ascent in the firm. Five years is the minimum for most people to be seen, heard, or recognized by upper management; a promotion is almost out of the question. However, Stephanie manages to move up the ladder in a year. Those whispers remain as hushes in the office because there's also a rumor that she will physically engage anyone who questions her position. Although there's no question that she possesses the brains, but her physical appearance raises eyebrows.

Stephanie is of a medium brown complexion, and her make-up is professionally done daily; her face stays beat to the gods. Green colored contacts and Brazilian bundles give her the look of exoticism she desires. Her slender 5'7 physique is accentuated by a voluptuous ass and a 36 B cup; she possesses the body and brains to get whatever and whomever she wants. Stephanie, or as her friends call her S.E.X., is all that, and she knows it. S.E.X. has a great life; money is no object for her, but it wasn't always like that. She grew up poor and was in an abusive marriage; that was enough for her to realize that she had to step up her game. To be the smart girl who was broke or beaten, was certainly out of the question. She learns that if she uses her body, she can get just as much, if not more. She is a beast in the bedroom, boardroom, or any room where she needs to get her point across. S.E.X. doesn't care who she steps over, steps on, or gets under to get what she wants. Money and material things are all that matters in her life. She lives in the most elegant estates known to man, pushes a

Porsche 911, and can easily drop two grands on a shopping spree during her lunch break. She does whatever, whenever, however, to whomever she wants. It's her world, and those in it should tread lightly.

S.E.X.is a cold, callous person who doesn't care if the "flavor of the month" is single, married, engaged, young, or old. It's funny though; she wasn't always like that. Behind the Brazilian weave, green contacts, and Christian Louis Vuitton shoes, is a severely wounded woman. Her hard demeanor is the result of years in an abusive relationship.

April 1988

Justin Xavier is a quiet, shy, and hard-working man. He believes in God, family, commitment, and dreams of being a provider for his future wife and kids. All Justin ever wanted in life was to be happy, meet the love of his life, and be a husband and a father. He and Stephanie met at a high school dance. In a crowd of mutual friends, Stephanie catches his eyes. There is something about this girl that separates her from the crowd. As soon as Justin gains the courage to go over and speak to her, gunfire rings out in the air, and everyone starts to scatter. In the midst of the wild crowd, Stephanie falls to the ground, and of course, all of her "friends" leave her. Justin notices this and quickly rushes to her side.

"Hello, beautiful. Do you need a hand?"

"I don't feel so beautiful from down here, but no, I think I can manage."

"Well, I'm Justin…Justin Xavier, and I assure you that you are the finest young lady out here."

"I'm Stephanie Baker, and I obviously have no real friends. I can't believe those skanks left me!"
Stephanie gathers herself from the ground and finally makes eye contact with Justin. It was like in the movies. Justin's 6'1, muscular build, and almond-shaped brown eyes, has her attention. She stands in a trance as he talks.

"Stephanie, a date? Do you think I can take you out?"

"Oh, what? I think that sounds good," she snapped out of the trance.

"How did you get here?"

"I walked with my so-called friends. I was supposed to go to a sleepover with them, but that's dead. I'll just walk home." "You don't have to walk; I can take you. My car is right over there." "I can't get in a car with you. I don't even know you." "Well, if you won't get in my car, I'll just have to walk you home. I won't let you walk alone." "I can't let you do that. If I ride with you, do you promise to take me straight home?" "I put it on everything I love. Stephanie, I'd put that on you because I already know I love you." That...Was... It! Justin has her hook, line, and sinker. He helps her into his car and starts to examine and brush her off to make sure she is okay. At this moment, Stephanie knows this man will be her husband. She thought to herself, *Finally, someone sees me, cares about me, and is trying to protect me.* It was indeed a mutual love at first sight.

Stephanie and Justin spent every single hour together, either talking on the phone, eating out, or hanging at each other's houses. They are joined at the hip. She truly loves him and gives him everything she has, even her virginity.

After three months, they make it known that they are a couple. It's Stephanie's 17th birthday, and Justin promises it will be a birthday she will never forget. He picks her up in his Toyota Celica sports car, and they go to dinner at Red Lobster. They walk in, and a hostess greets them and walks them to a booth near the back of the restaurant. Stephanie slides in and Justin sits next to her. Not long after, a waitress comes to the table and takes their order.

"Hello, my name is Barbara, and I will be your server for this evening. Can I get the both of you started with a glass of water while you review the menu?" Justin instantly replies, "That will be great, thank you." "Okay, we just took some cheddar bay biscuits out of the oven; I will bring you a basket when I return with your water," Barbara mentions.

As Barbara walks away to retrieve our water and biscuits, Justin reviews the menu and on the other hand, I am having a hard time concentrating because I'm so nervous. As Justin leans in to kiss me, Barbara returns with our water. After Barbara tells us the specials, we place our orders. I keep thinking about how much time I want to spend with Justin outside of the restaurant. I ordered the she-crab soup and a salad, but Justin, on the other hand, ordered a Seagram's Seven, a T-bone steak, shrimps, baked potato, and a side salad.

"Justin, it's so nice in here."

"I'm glad you like it; only the best for my baby."

He leans over, gently caresses Stephanie's face and leans in for a kiss since Barbara interrupted the first one. It is a long passionate kiss. When he pulls away, Stephanie puckered her lips for more. He comes back in and does it again. The passion that flows between them is undeniable. When the kiss ends, Stephanie has butterflies.

"Steph, I love you."

"I know you do."

"No, I don't think you really understand how much I really love you."

"Justin, I do understand because I love you the same."

"I want you to know that I want to make love to you, but only if you're ready."

"We've talked about this, and I told you that I'm ready."

"I don't want to pressure you into anything; I want you to want it too."

"I do. I want to give myself to you today, tomorrow, and forever, as long as you will have me in your life."

They stare into one another's eyes, and Justin grabs and rubs Stephanie's hand. The gaze is broken when the waiter brings out their food.

"Let me know if you two need anything else."

"We will," Justin responds.

Justin eats his food as a man starved, but Stephanie can hardly eat. Her mind is on what's about to happen after dinner. Will it hurt? Will she cry? Will Justin be gentle? All kinds of questions rush through her mind as she tries to nibble on her food.

"Are you alright Steph? I thought you were hungry."

"I'm fine. I just don't feel so hungry after all."

"If you want, we can leave."

"Eat your food; I love how you chew on those shrimps." They both laugh at what Stephanie said. Justin finishes his food, and Barbara brings the bill. Justin pays, and the two leave hand and hand. Next stop...Motel 6. Justin reserves a suite at Motel 6 (and yep, they left the light on!). The room had flowers, candles, and wine. It was the first time in my life that I didn't dread being on this earth, yet another year. As we walk into the motel, I smiled because he took the time to decorate the room for the occasion, with flowers, wine, and fake candles. In my mind he was treating me better than anyone else ever had before. My hands began to shake as I walked over to the bed. Justin instantly started taking off his shoes. When he finished, he reaches out his hand to me, I was stuck in one spot, not really sure what to do, or how to do it. How I wished I had someone to forewarn me so I would have been prepared. As Justin grabs my hand and starts to caress it as well as my arm, I could tell he was experienced with this sort of thing. I mean, after all he was older, street smart, and confident, so all I could do was close my eyes and follow along. He slowly started kissing me and it was welcomed and desired. I love the way he smells, feels, and tastes. I could kiss him forever. As my mind is so fixated on his tongue and lips, he is gliding his hands under my stonewashed mini skirt. I'm wet between my legs (almost too wet)-*I hope my period didn't start-I have at least 3 more days-shit!* Justin moves to the bed and pulls me down. As he slid his fingers in my pussy all I could say was, "mmm" and in the midst of letting my guard down my body begins to relax, my eyes are closed and my legs are slowly spreading apart...almost like an out-of-body experience.

"Just relax" he whispers.

Too shocked to speak, I just nod my head. He starts taking off his clothes, but I'm too zoned out to move, as he pulls his pants and boxers down, I see his dick; it's hard and ready. *It's beautiful-damn-why didn't I pay attention to my friends- (it would have been nice to know what to do with it).* He gets up off the bed and stands in front of me and strokes it back and forth slowly at first. He closed his eyes and let out a low moan. Just above a demanding whisper he says, "Kiss it." My mouth drops open-*it's beautiful-yes, but it's also gross-I mean he didn't even wash it.* I try to play it off like I didn't hear him. He steps closer and says it again.

"No, I'm not doing that."

"Don't you love me? Do it this one time baby." He begs. As I lean in to kiss the tip, my lip touches this sticky stuff coming from it. "Yuk," I say as I am wiping my mouth.

Chuckling he says, "Don't worry, he was introducing himself."

That shit was not funny.

"Take off your clothes and get under the covers. I will help you relax."

"Umm ok" I utter.

"Nice." He mentioned. "Turn off the lamp and just relax." As I try to oblige, he removes his shirt and slides under the covers next to me. His touch is soft and gentle. I'm not sure if he is nervous, excited, worried, or just being a typical guy. Justin kissed my arms, my shoulders, he traveled up my neck, but before he kissed my lips, he places a kiss on my forehead. This sensual move brought tears to my eyes. I had always heard a man who really loves you will kiss you on your forehead. At that moment, I touched him, and his naked body felt small but strong. I wanted to feel his body on me and most defiantly feel all of him inside of me. Once again Justin toyed with my pussy; he slid his finger up and down my clit. Apparently he wanted to toy with my mind and body by making me beg so he started inserting his fingers in my pussy one at a time... two fingers in, Justin could feel my inner body pulsate, so he quickly pulled his fingers out and circled them around my clit once again. He kept doing this until I was about to explode with anticipation. I tried grabbing his arm so he could put his fingers back in my warm wet spot, but he refused to play along. Without notice, Justin climbed on the top of me, and within a blink; he took the tip of his penis and tried to insert it in my pussy.

"WAIT!! STOP!!" I screamed.

"Just wait, it's going to be okay." He reassures me. "Just hold on to me tight, it will all be inside of you in a minute."

"OOWW...NO... PLEASE..."

He leans down to kiss me-hoping this will help me to relax.

I am screaming and at the same time trying to be a woman. I know this pain is only momentarily, but at this moment, all I feel is pain, but right when I was in the midst of asking him to stop (yet again), things started to feel good, almost perfect. As my movement began to mimic his, I began to feel love, wanted, needed, and a new woman. Justin's pace quickens and I kept thinking the bed was going to break. He lifts both of my legs in the air and starts to hammer me until both of us cum simultaneously.

Oh my God!

My legs are worthless at this second, so Justin helps me and then he collapses on top of me. As we work to catch our breath, I am trapped under his body, but I refuse to say anything; I just want to feel this love connection forever. *BEST BIRTHDAY EVER!!!*

Justin and I made love, and it was EVERYTHING! He felt me, he touched me, he every part of my body, and for the first time, I understood the reason why all my friends were so boy crazy. Justin made me cry, scream, climax (over, and over again), and made me feel loved.

In the middle of the night, Justin goes outside to smoke

a cigarette, so I decide to hop in the shower. When I came out of the bathroom, the atmosphere shifted in the room. It is cold, quiet, and still. Too quiet and still. Justin has a look on his face that's a bit scary, but a little sexy at the same time. Slowly, I approach him with my towel wrapped around me, he stands up and slaps the hell out of me.

"Aaaaaa!" I screamed.

I fly onto the bed and before I could move, he jumps on me and starts to choke me. I fight for air, my dignity, and my life. And no lie, just like the light Motel 6 left on outside of their establishment, the light went on in his head. In one swift move, he stops; he sits down in a chair located in the corner of the room.

"Are you trying to kill me? You know how much I love you!" He yelled.

I sit there. I'm confused and the tears that just recently came from pleasure now fall down my face from the pain.

In a calm voice, he asks, "Who is Eric?"

In between shock and confusion, I question, "Eric?"

He yelled, "YES, WHO THE FUCK IS ERIC? Are you playing games with me? Your pager went off, so I called the number back and some punk mutherfucker named Eric was on the phone asking for you."

Now I'm really confused. The only Eric I know is my neighbor, and I never gave that fool my pager number. As I try to collect my thoughts it apparently takes me too long to answer.

WHACK!!

Justin punches me in my head, I'm in flight mode; I've never been in a fight, so that was not an option. I need to get out of this situation. As I gather my clothes, I have a conversation with myself. I know I must devise an exit plan, but heck at this point the only plan is put on my clothes and walk, no, RUN out of the door. Amid the conversation with myself, Justin starts to cry, and apologize. He begs me to please forgive him and not leave.

Sigh. Is this love? Is this what I need to endure to be with someone? Is it really worth it? Apparently, this is what God had in the cards for me.

I forgive him, and we have sex. —just sex, (I vowed, I would never make love to another man ever again). A year later, we go to the Justice of the Peace to get married; we both promise to never speak of that night ever again. His vow to me is to never hit me again, and to always protect me for the rest of my life. This is the biggest lie ever told. Although Stephanie loves Justin with every fiber of her being, he doesn't reciprocate or spare the rod. He beats her daily and mercilessly. In this relationship, she learns that love isn't enough to bring happiness. Justin was the man of her dreams when they met, but now he is her worst nightmare. Time proves to be an enemy the longer Stephanie stays with him. Justin's love for her proves to be short-lived. The only thing he loves is himself and his Seagram's 7, straight (no chaser). Stephanie knows she'll never have the picket fence with 2 kids, and the dog. After one of his vicious tirades, he beat Stephanie so badly that she miscarried their twins. That is the finale. She flees for her life. Stephanie leaves memories of him, her lost babies, and her submissive self where they all belong--in the past.

Kelsey

"Thank you for calling William and Wilson's Law Firm, Kelsey Simmons speaking, how can I help you?" The person on the other end speaks.

She smiles and replies, "Oh shit, my panties just got wet, I will be there in 20 minutes!"

Kelsey hangs up the phone and in one swift move; she grabbed her purse and her keys and ran out of her office.

"Hey Kelsey, I was coming to your office to speak to you about..."

I tried to say as Kelsey rushes past me.

"Not now...pill working!"

"What?" I asked.

"Look girl, I gotta go. Schedule an appointment and I will be back in 2... no, make that 3 hours."

"What?"

Kelsey steps close to Stephanie and whispered, "Look, Bitch, my husband hasn't been able to perform in a week, he took a blue pill and the shit has kicked in, I got to go, NOW MOVE!" I shake my head, laugh, and step to the side.

Kelsey Simmons is head of the marketing department at William & Wilson Law Firm. She stands 5'4 and is sure to be heard before she's seen. She can be your best friend or your worst enemy. The girl is straight hood but worked day and night to put herself through college; she has no problem reminding anyone of that accomplishment. She is happily married to her high school sweetheart, Barry Simmons. They have two amazing children and live in a predominately white neighborhood. She is truly living her best life. Kelsey and Stephanie met at the law firm and have been friends ever since. Stephanie recalls thinking how refreshing it was to see another black woman at the table in the boardroom, so their friendship was a given. They eat lunch together and as the years went by, they considered themselves, sisters from another mister.

Stephanie thanks God every day for Kelsey. No one knows her secrets except Kelsey, so it's definitely important to always keep her in her corner no matter how many times she questions why she puts up with Kelsey's ghetto mentality. She knows Kelsey is the only person who would punch a nigga in the face first and ask questions later. Don't let Kelsey's title, her "Becky" voice, or the fact that her husband is the lieutenant at the local police department fool you. Kelsey is THAT GIRL!

Stephanie

■ had been working hard at my desk for hours, when I finally looked up from my computer, and noticed Kelsey sashaying by with a smile on her face. Glancing at the clock, I noticed that four hours had passed by, *hmm I guess the blue pill worked*, I thought to myself. Needing answers to some documents I was working on, I decide to go to Kelsey's office.

"Hey Kelsey."

"Hellooo Huntie."

Yep the blue pills worked. I thought to myself and smirked.

"I need the final numbers on that Grayson's account you have been working on so I can close the case."

"Chile please leave my office if you are here to discuss work."

"Kelsey, I don't have time to play with you, you are holding me up from closing out my month-end cases, now stop playing around and give me the damn numbers."

"Pump your brakes 'lil girl," Kelsey said as she swiftly moves around her desk. "I will give you the damn numbers when I am done, now get yo ass out of my office."

"What the fuck is your problem?"

"Right this second, you are my problem, now leave!"

I left her office more pissed and confused, *I guess the blue pills didn't work after all.* I chuckled to myself. I stayed clear of Kelsey for the remainder of the day. By 6:00 pm, I decided to call it a day and head home to relax and unwind. *Maybe I can call someone to work out the kinks in my back, and ease some of the tension in my body... sounds tempting.* I was so deep in thought that I didn't notice Kelsey waiting at the elevator.

"Hey girl," Kelsey said.

In mid-step I stopped, and quickly looked behind me to see who Kelsey was referring to, but to my dismay no one was there.

"Hey." "Look, I want to apologize about the situation earlier, I will have the information that you need first thing in the morning."

"No need to apologize." I mentioned, "But is everything okay with you and Barry?"

"Yes, everything is fine, why do you ask?"

"No reason, just asking."

"So, you want to go out for a drink?" Kelsey asked.

"No, I think I will take a rain check, I just want to go home and relax."

Kelsey grabs my arm and begs, "Stephanie, I really could use some company right now. Please let's go out and have a drink. I will even pay the bill."

Sigh.

"In that case, sure let's go," I replied.

Kelsey puts the biggest smile on her face, pushes the down button for the elevator, and starts to do the Holy Ghost shout. I fell out laughing.

With tears in my eyes, I say, "Kelsey, you are one crazy bitch."

And just like that, all has been forgotten and forgiven between the two.

The Red Rooster is a cozy jazz bar around the corner from the office. They usually have a live jazz band that plays there several nights a week. It is a place where you can go to relax and unwind with a nice cocktail, great food, and soothing music. A place where you can sit back and enjoy as the stress from the day slowly eases away. Several of the employees from the office frequent the bar, so of course, Stephanie and Kelsey never have to wait for a seat, regardless of how packed the place is, and that is usually every night.

"Hey ladies," Donna, the hostess cheerfully says, "you ladies are looking beautiful as always. Would you like your usual table?"

"Aww Donna, you are so sweet, thank you for the compliment," Kelsey says. "When are you going to let us steal you from this place and bring you over to the world of Corporate America?" "Never... I see how stressed you two always look when you come in there, no ma'am, I am not interested in that world at all!"

The jazz music floating around the room was smooth and sexy, the drinks were fabulous, and the atmosphere was exactly what the doctor ordered. Kelsey and I continued to ignore the elephant in the room about the earlier incident in the office, but heck if she is good with the situation, then so am I, I thought to myself. Donna approached our table with another round of drinks but before she placed them on the table Kelsey or I should say, Ghetto K, jumps up and yells, "HEY, HEY-we did not order these and I'm not fit 'tin to pay for them!"
Donna throws her hands up and surrenders, "Slow your roll Kelsey, these are compliments from the gentleman at the bar."

"Tell him to keep his drinks, a girl is paid and can supply her own alcohol." Before Donna could move, I politely removed both drinks from the tray and held one up to the chocolate drop at the bar. *Smile-Wink-Sip.* In between my sips, I tell Kelsey and Donna I can pay for my drinks as well but free is always better.

Donna smiles and walks away.

"You are such a slut," Kelsey mentions.

"Yep, a slut with two free drinks."

"Keep it up, one day you are going to meet your match."

I began to sway back and forth to the music. *She will not fuck up my free buzz.*

"Kelsey, I have already met my match. Her name is Kelsey Simmons and that bitch is crazy as fuck!"

Kelsey gasp in shock, but before she could respond, the chocolate drop from the bar is standing at our table.

Damn!

Kelsey looks him up and down and yells, "Jesus take the wheel; you are so sexy!" I could not agree more but at least I kept my thoughts to myself. Acknowledging her, he smiles and gently nods his head. He extends his hand to introduce himself. Cedric Armstrong is 6 feet 4 inches, chocolate skin, brown piercing eyes, and one dimple on his right cheek when he smiles, and man oh man, the prettiest set of white teeth I have ever seen in my entire life. He has the body of a football player, tall, solid, and fit. The dirty thoughts that are running through my mind right now are truly making my kitten purr. I need his face buried in the middle of my pussy right-about-now. He is telling me about himself but I have no clue what he is saying, I heard something about work, visiting a colleague, and in town for a few days, but all I can think about is how good his dick might taste, no correction, will taste in my mouth. I just need to get one good fuck to get me back on track, and to be honest Mr. Armstrong seems to be the man of the hour. As I focus to bring myself back to reality, he is handing me his business card and suggests that we finish this conversation tomorrow over dinner and drinks.

Shit, no dick tonight? Sigh.

I agree and told him I will call him later to discuss the plans. As he turns to leave, I noticed Kelsey has a strange look on her face that totally ruined my buzz. *Shit, party over.*

"Well Steph," Kelsey says in between a yawn. "I'm going to call it a night, be sure to call me when you arrive home."

As I lean in to hug her, I agreed and decided to call it a night as well. I quickly scan the bar to wave goodbye to Cedric. The fresh air and warm breeze outside kissed me on the cheek, I did not realize how stuffy the bar was, but the cool spring air was refreshing. Walking to my car, my thoughts flashed back to how erratic Kelsey has been acting over the last few days, as I make a mental note to schedule a girl's spa day for us, as soon as possible.

Meanwhile...

Kelsey

As Kelsey is driving north on Piney Street, her mind is consumed, her heart is racing, and she has the biggest smile on her face. As the old school slow jams are playing on the radio all she is focused on is getting the love and attention she needs right now. Pulling up at the Crowne Plaza, she parks and quickly exits her vehicle. As she approaches room 215 her heart is beating a hundred miles an hour. There was no need to knock because she had her own key. You see room 215 was their special room. In fact, room 215 has been her room every week for the last few months. Yep, you guessed it Kelsey has been living a double life, but as the saying goes, what goes on in the dark will surely come out in the light.

Stephanie

I called Kelsey to let her know I made it home, but the call went to voicemail. "Hmm that is weird." *Well I did my part.* Stephanie has always been the responsible one for as long as she could remember. Having to raise herself since she was 10 years old, doing the right thing became second nature to her. She can remember days of having to beg for food from the neighbors so she could eat, because her mother felt crack was more important to her than her daughter. As a young child, Stephanie began to know the tricks of the trade. In school she would fake a headache so she could go to the nurse's office to get a sandwich and a nap. When her mother didn't pay the light bill, she would be too afraid to go to sleep because she never knew what was lurking in the dark. Or when her mother would use the welfare check to splurge on an extra rock rather than pay the water bill Stephanie would get to school earlier than the other students so she could take a birdie in the girls' bathroom. There were a few times when she would purposely pour milk on her clothes so she could go to lost 'n' found and get a new outfit. Stephanie has come from a rough life and refuses to ever go back to being poor. She never knew her father and at this point in her life she could care less if her mother was dead or alive. Those days no longer exists in her mind. As much as she wants to be a wife and mother, those things require time, patience, love, and a caring heart...all those things she no longer has, nor desire. Having someone else's man was a lot less stressful than having a man to call her own. Love 'em and leave 'em - what more can a girl ask for—NOTHING. Happiness is a word that is meant for everyone, except Stephanie.

Kelsey

Kelsey arrives at the job extra early so she could get the Grayson account finalized so she could pass the information on to Stephanie. She did not like how things went down in the office the day before, that's why she felt the need to make amends and go out for drinks last night. A sly smile suddenly appeared on her face as she reflects on the sexcapade she had last night. *What would people think if they found out what I am doing?* Shaking her head to remove the thoughts, the smirk suddenly disappeared, and a single tear rolled down her left cheek. How could she feel so good and yet feel so bad all at the same time? Kelsey knew what happened last night eventually would have to come to an end, but she constantly desires to feel like a true woman. She could not forget the feeling of his dick in her hand, her mouth, her pussy, and her asshole. She started to shiver with excitement; suddenly Kelsey felt an overwhelming desire to relive the feeling. Since she was the only one in the office, she glides her hands down to her wet pulsating vagina and inserted two fingers, as she let out a quick short breath, she closed her eyes and lived in the moment. Her slow movement started to accelerate and before she knew it Kelsey exploded but instead of removing her fingers she began rubbing her clit; she needed to cum again, but she needed to be stimulated, so she reached in her bottom desk drawer and pulled out her curling iron. Moving her thong to the side, she spread her legs and inserts the barrel. As her pussy quivers and her legs shake, a thought of DaShawn's face appears in her mind.

Stephanie

I woke up feeling drained. I honestly wanted to call in sick and just kick back and enjoy the sunny weather. Instead I decided to take a stroll in my backyard for some fresh air. As the sun glistened off the water in the pool, I noticed how inviting and refreshing it looked so without hesitation, I dropped my robe and leaped in the pool. Swimming has always been my favorite past time. The idea of not having to be, do, or think is always a welcomed part of my day. After completing five laps I figured it was time to get dressed and head into the office. I was feeling a bit refreshed and feisty, so I decided to wear my Jovani red two-piece business suit and my black Jimmy Choo pumps. As I grabbed my purse to fish for my keys, I came across Cedric's business card, and before I could second guess myself, I grabbed my cell phone and dialed his number.

"Cedric Armstrong speaking." He said.

"Hi Cedric, it's S.E.X.-I mean Stephanie." As I exhaled, I didn't realize I was holding my breath.

"Oh, hello beautiful, how is your day going?"

Smiling I replied, "Pretty good, thank you for asking."

"I am glad you called. So, does this mean you are going take me up on my offer?"

"What offer?"

"Dinner before I leave town."

"Oh, dinner, right. Umm that might work."

"How about tonight? I can swing by your office after work, maybe around 5?" He questions.

"Yes, that will work. I will text you the address."

"Great! I look forward to seeing you later today."

"Bye," I said with a smile on my voice.

I hung up the phone, grabbed my purse, and floated out of the house. I automatically knew it was going to be a great day, and with any luck it will be an even better night.

Stephanie

On my way into the office, I made a mental note to stop by the lingerie store on my lunch break so I could pick up something, just in case I needed it after my dinner date with Cedric.

Stephanie's mind wondered back to a time when she worked at the lingerie store before getting an internship at the law firm. Gerald was the first person who introduced her to a life of rough sex. As Stephanie reflects on that night, she wondered whatever happened to Gerald.

February 2005

After the horrible life with Justin, I did not think I would ever enjoy sex, or the art of falling in love again that is until I met Gerald. Before I started at the law firm, I worked part-time at a lingerie store and Gerald came in needing some assistance. He was cute; he had that country boy swagger about himself with the cutest smile in the world. Pearly whites that could be seen from miles away, wow, nothing like a man with a great smile. Even though the wedding band was blinding on his finger, I knew I wanted him, and I was not going to let a minor detail like his wife get in my way.

"Excuse me," he said, "Can you tell me does this teddy come in a size 10?"

"No, sorry it doesn't, but it does come in a size 3, which happens to be my size, and I am sure you would like to see it on me way more than you would on your size 10 wife." As the smile grew bigger on his face, so did the bulge in his pants. *Jackpot I think to myself.*

"Let me show you what we do have in a size 10 and then you can buy both, that way all four of us will be happy."

He questions, "Four of us?"

"Yes," I said. "You, me, your wife, and my soon to be new friend, Harry."

The smile disappears, "Harry?" "Yes." As I approach him even closer- so close I can smell the peppermint gum he is chewing.

"Harry is the bulge in your pants that I am dying to kiss."

The smile returns. *Double jackpot.*

"Well I would hate to disappoint Harry so I will take all four of them."

"Four?"

"Yes, your teddy, her teddy, your name and your number." He smiles.

Damn, my body starts to tingle. Hell, if he does that with his clothes on, I can't wait to get him naked. I silently pray, *"Dear God, please forgive me for the sins I am about to commit with this country boy, but God, you shouldn't have sent him in this store so technically this is Your fault."*

Gerald and I spoke several times over the next couple of days on the phone, and finally decided to meet so he could enjoy the teddy he so graciously purchased for me. He came overbearing flowers and wine and I came to the door wearing the teddy he purchased.

"Nice place," he says.

My mouth says thanks, but my mind is thinking about how he should be looking at my half-naked body and not my furniture. I see the country boy is going to be a little extra work. *Touché God, you win.*

Gerald and I sat on separate couches having mindless conversation. I wanted to just fuck him and send him on his way, but apparently, the country boy was very nervous, and from what I could see extra country with a side of boring. As I sat there listening to him talk about nothing, well at least it's nothing to me… all I could think about was how I gave up a night of shopping for this shit. At least the wine he brought was good because it is truly working right now.

As Gerald continues to ramble on about his kids, his wife, and his job my mind drifts once again on my midterm exam. *I need to make sure I pass this exam if I want to have an opportunity at getting an internship at William & Wilson's Law Firm. I know if I get an opportunity to at least get my foot in the door, I can make wonders happen for my career.*

"What?" I asked.

"So, do you want to move this conversation to the bedroom?"

Think Stephanie...think... if he is as boring in the bedroom as he is in the living room, I am going to slit my wrist.

"Umm, you know it is getting kind of late, shouldn't you be getting home to your wife?"

"Are you sure that is what you want?"

Hell no, I wanted to have at least been put to sleep by now from a big dick and not from boredom.

"Well it is getting kind of late and I have an early class tomorrow."

"Oh, okay, well it was good chatting with you." He says.

Really? Well at least one of us had a good time.

"Yes, it was good chatting." *(Fake smile and yawn)* "We must do this again." *Never ever again in my life.* And then he does it...he grabs me, kisses me, and lets his fingers explore the teddy that he bought. In between the gasp and moans I instantly forget how boring he was and how this night was almost a waste. Gerald slips his fingers in my wet pussy and like butter; they slide right in and hit my spot. I smile inside and out. As he continues to kiss me on my neck, I began aggressively pulling his shirt off. I needed him inside of me right now. I forced my hands down his pants and all I could think about was how thick his dick was and how I wanted to taste it and swallow all his future kids. Before I could move any further, in one swift move, Gerald throws me over his shoulders and takes me upstairs to my bedroom. As I direct him to the room, I am suddenly debating if I want him to wear a condom or if I want to feel all his natural thickness. My pussy starts to pulsate at just the thought of him putting his penis head in my pussy. As he throws me on the bed, I reach out to him.

"Gerald, I want you to fuck me so bad."

"Are you sure you want this?" He questions as he spreads my legs apart.

"Yes, I am sure."

His home life is not the best and with a size 10 wife, sex is not even close to what he desires. It had been a long time since he was pleased in the bedroom. Without hesitation, he lowers his head between my legs, and slowly starts to move his tongue up and down my clit. Gerald is determined to make sure Stephanie remembers this night for a long time. In fact, he hopes that he can make her fall in love with him so he can have sex on a regular basis.

Gerald licked and sucked all my juices. Before I could even think about a condom, he rammed his dick into my vagina. I wanted to say something, heck anything, but all I could do was enjoy how good Gerald was fucking me. He sucked on my titties, bit my nipples, and then he did the one thing that took me to pure ecstasy; he choked me and told me to beg for more. At first, I started to panic, because all the abuse from Justin flashed back into my mind, but this chocking was different. It was good, it was intense, it was sexy as fuck. And I did exactly what he told him to do; I begged for more, and in the midst of that night of fucking we climaxed at the same time. Gerald collapsed on top of me, our breathing became one and suddenly the tears slowly slid down my cheek. Not sure what was happening to my mind and my body, I quickly pushed Gerald off me and rolled on my side.

"Are you okay?" He asks as he reached for me.

"Yes, I'm fine; it's time for you to go."

"What? Why?"

"I just think it would be best."

"Did I hurt you?"

Silence

"Stephanie, please talk to me. I only did what you asked me to do." Silence.

"What can I do to make it up to you?" He asks. "Please talk to me." He begs. As I move off the bed and grabbed my robe, I now recall the fact that he is someone else's man and will never be mine.

Gerald is no longer needed, he fucked her, and he will never get this opportunity again. Stephanie pushes every man away. One and done and yep, Gerald's time was up.

"Gerald, this can never happen again. Leave my house. I never want to see you again."

"But..."

Get-out" I mentioned through clenched teeth.

And without another thought, dazed and confused Gerald puts his clothes on and follows her down the stairs with no explanation as to what happened and why. Stephanie walks him down the stairs and without any eye contact; she opens the front door and waits patiently as Gerald walks out.

"Stephanie, please talk to me. I want to see you again, please just tell me what I did wrong?"

I quickly slammed the door and on cue the tears began to fall. I fell to my knees and curses the day I was born. I cursed Justin, God, my crack head mother, but most of all; I cursed Gerald for leaving with a piece of my heart.

"God why can't I have the life I desire?" "Why are others worthy of what I deserve?"

Tired and exhausted, I climbed the stairs back to my bedroom, and as I laid there reliving the night; I reached over and inhaled the scent that Gerald left on my pillowcase. My mind raced back to the way he choked me and the way it made me feel inside. Before I drifted off to sleep, I reminded myself to research *the art of choking during sex,* and I definitely convince myself, I will get that internship by any means necessary. *I might have to see if his phone number still works.* She thought to herself. Because of that night, she is who she is today. If Gerald never came into her life, she might not have ever pushed herself as hard at the firm when she tried out for the intern position.

Kelsey

Kelsey had the hardest time concentrating at work. Every little thing worked her nerves: the phone; the happy people passing by, and the constant message alert on her cell phone had her on the verge of throwing her phone in the trash. Barry was not happy with the time she arrived home the previous night, and of course she did not give him an explanation. Early on in their marriage, she made a rule, don't ask and your feelings won't get hurt. Kelsey was raised by her aunt and uncle, not because of bad parents, but because her parents wanted her to have a better life; you see, Kelsey was always pampered and treated like a princess. She always had that no-nonsense attitude towards people. Kelsey was always popular in high school because she knew how to hold her own, so when Barry came into her life, he was wanted and not needed, because Kelsey never needed anything...her life was put together. Barry had to learn where, when, and how to fit in if he wanted to be with her, and of course he accepted the challenge. Inside of the home, Barry's job was to provide and protect - no more/no less; Kelsey's job was to do the rest, so coming home at 3:00 am was not up for discussion. Kelsey loved Barry with everything that she has, but right now Barry's providing and protecting was not enough to keep her happy.

KNOCK-KNOCK

"Come in," Kelsey sighs.

"Hey girl, how are you? How was your night?" I quizzed.

Sounding defeated, "Hey sis, I'm good, a bit tired but no complaints. Sorry I didn't call you back last night, it was a long night."

"Is everything okay?"

"Girl yes, I came in early to finish the report you needed," Kelsey mentions as she hands the report to Stephanie. "If you have any questions, please let me know."

"Okaayyy." I said with a confused look on my face.

While walking out of the office, I turn and mentioned, "You know I'm here for you if you ever need anything...ever."

And right there in the midst of sensitivity, Ghetto K chimes in, "Bitch unless you got a big dick, there is nothing I need from you."

I gasped and replied, "Fuck you Kelsey."

"Again, NO DICK...NO THANK YOU!"

I playfully throw a paperclip at Kelsey and laugh as I walk out of her office. Kelsey sits in her chair and turns to enjoy the view outside. IF only she could open the window and enjoy the breeze that awaits her outside-but on the other hand, thank God she can't open the window-she might jump. What would people say if (more like) when all the truth comes out? Her mother who is a pastor, by the way, will splash holy oil on her and start speaking in tongues, her husband might shoot her, her kids will disown her, DaShawn would be there with the biggest smile on his face, but in Kelsey's heart the thrill would be gone if the truth came out, and Stephanie...well Stephanie might high-five her for being a slut. Life could be so much easier if she just disappeared. All her hard work to be a good wife, daughter, mother, and best friend has now put a heavyweight on Kelsey, mentally, emotionally, and physically. Not only is Kelsey cheating on her husband but she has been battling breast cancer-or the scare of breast cancer. A few months ago, her mammogram biopsy came back inconclusive and she refuses to go back for more testing. She has made it up in her mind that not knowing is the best diagnosis for her right now. Her final day may be close or far away, but until she is ready to hear the results, she will continue to live her life on the edge. As she brings her thoughts back to reality, Kelsey sends a quick text message to Stephanie.

Kelsey: *Wanna play hooky and escape for the rest of the day?*

Stephanie: *Can't... date with Cedric after work.*

Kelsey: *Who in da hell is Cedric?*

Stephanie: *Chocolate drop from the bar last night.*

Kelsey: *SLUT (cursing emoji)*

Stephanie: *PUNK (side eye emoji)*

Kelsey: *See if he has a brother so we can double date...*

Stephanie: *WTF*

Kelsey: *JK! Be safe tonight. Do I need to do a rescue call?*

Stephanie: *Please do because cute sometimes turns to crazy.*

Kelsey: *Will run interference at 8:00 pm. Love you.*

Stephanie: *LY2.*

Running interference was always something Kelsey did when Stephanie went out on dates. This would help her get out of a bad, boring, or crazy date when needed. *Hell, I wish I had her life.* Kelsey thought. *But since I don't, I will continue to enjoy the young tenderoni I have right now.* "Oh well Kelsey, back to work!" She says to no one in particular. Her cell phone vibrates, and a joker smile appears on her face, but instead of answering hello like normal people, Kelsey answers, "I'm on my way, and the dick betta be hard and ready."

Smiling as she hangs up the phone, grabs her purse, and sashays out of the office. She closes her office door and tells the receptionist to cancel all her appointments for the rest of the day, and to have a good weekend.

Kelsey had personal business to handle!

Stephanie

The day had been a blur for me. Since I was a top-notch customer at my favorite lingerie store, I went online and ordered a sexy nightgown, and had them deliver it to the office. The thought of possibly getting some past due dick was all I desired right now. I felt bad because I couldn't spend time with Kelsey, but I needed to finish my work and keep my mind clear and ready for Mr. Armstrong. I smiled at the thought of him, his sexy voice, broad shoulders, and a smile that would take all my troubles away. Suddenly, I felt my face heat up, in the midst of drinking water to cool myself off; there was a soft tap on my office door.

"Yes?"

I'm a little early, but I couldn't wait to see you." Cedric says as he slides in the office and hands me a dozen pink roses.

"Aww thank you, Cedric, these are beautiful." I beamed as I inhaled the fresh scent.

"So, do you need a few minutes to finish your work?"

"Oh no, not at all...Actually I haven't been very productive today." I said as I avoided his piercing eyes. Logging off of my computer and grabbing my purse and my shopping bag, I continued to avoid his presence; his cologne has me in a trance. *Get it together S.E.X., he is just a man.* He opens the door for me and steps to the side so I could pass.

"Well look at you, such a gentleman." I flirt.

"A gentleman by day and a freak by night." He whispers in her ear.

GASP "Well I might have to test your theory."

"I hope you do." His eyes twinkled as he smiled.

Clearing my throat, I quickly change the subject, "So have you picked a place for dinner?"

"My colleague recommends Ruth Chris, but if you have a better idea, I'm game."

"Well to be honest, I'm sure you're tired of always eating out. If you promise to behave, why don't you follow me to my house and let me make you a home-cooked meal."

"You cook?" He asked with a doubtful look on his face. "I mean no offense, but you don't look like you know the first thing about a kitchen."

The smile disappears from my face, "So first a gentleman and then an ass huh?" I mentioned as I pushed away from him. "Forget about dinner and take your stink flowers back you damn jerk."

Totally in shock Cedric rushes to catch me and grabs me by my arm and quickly apologizes.

"Hey, hey, I'm sorry. I did not mean anything negative by that, please accept my apology."

He reached down to touch my face and once again the heat rises in my body. He leans in to kiss me on my cheek.

"Do you forgive me? I was only saying you are too sexy to be in the kitchen."

Inhaling his cologne, I quickly forgive him, hell I am trying to get some overdue dick, so there is no time to be upset.

"You are forgiven but consider this your strike one." I smiled, even though I am actually serious. "Two more and I block your ass via phone, email, and any and all other communication."

"I suppose I can respect that." He said with a slight chuckle.

"Anyway, here is my address, just in case we get separated on the way to the house."

"Trust me, I can keep up with you, but I will take it just in case," He says as he hands her the bouquet of flowers back and leads her to the elevator.

I suddenly feel butterflies in the pit of my stomach.

This is going to be a tough one. I think to myself.

I bet she is a beast in the bedroom, he thought.

The chemistry between the two of them is magical, intense, and oh so sexy. When they approached the main door to the building, Stephanie waved goodbye and rushed to her car. She is seriously cursing herself for volunteering to cook for this guy, but the idea of spending time in a restaurant would only prolong getting him back to her place. It's rare and I do mean very rare Stephanie cooks but trust and believe she can definitely throw down in a kitchen. Her signature meal is smothered pork chops, rice, green beans, and corn muffins, but tonight she will make another one of her favorites; shrimp and grits. That is another southern meal that is sure to put anyone to sleep. She will give him just enough to get him full; putting him to sleep will be her job tonight.

Once they arrive at her place, she welcomes Cedric in and told him to make himself at home. He of course grabs the remote and turns to ESPN. *Typical man-sigh.* Paying him no mind, Stephanie goes into the kitchen and pours a glass of wine while she gets started on dinner.

"Would you like a beer, wine or something stronger?" I yelled from the kitchen, but before I could finish my question, Cedric appears in the doorway.

"Sure, I will have what you are having." He smiles.

There goes that damn smile again. Handing him a glass, I say, "Help yourself."

"Are you sure I can't help you with anything? I do know my way around the kitchen, as well."

"Oh, so you're trying to get me to take your strike back?"

"Is it working?"

"NOPE!" I slightly giggle.

"So, I have a question," Cedric mentioned.

"Umm okay," I replied with a puzzled look on my face.

"When you called me today, you referred to yourself as SEX, is there something I need to know?"

"Yes, actually you do, I was telling you what I need." I chuckled.

"Ohhh, is that right?" He questioned.

"You really are a guy!" I chuckled again, "No, S.E.X. are my initials, most of my friends call me that."

"Interesting, because if it is something you need I can and will oblige." He says in a deep husky voice.

Before I could respond, he closed the gap and kissed me. Our tongues dance, our bodies are pressed together, and his hands start to explore my body. I could feel the length of his penis inside his business suit.

Pushing him back so I could catch my breath, I tell him, "I need to get back to preparing dinner."

"I would rather eat you." He whispers.

Without another word, I turned off the stove, grabbed his hand, and pulled him to my bedroom.

Suck it!" Cedric said as his manhood stood directly in my face. "Tell me you want and need this dick."

I sucked it like this was the last dick on earth. As I closed my eyes I slowly glided inch by inch in my mouth trying not to gag, I feel his dick getting harder by the second. The more I sucked the more aroused I became. I released his dick and began sliding my tongue and hands up towards his chest. As he laid there-spread eagle with his eyes closed and a slight smile on his face. I decided to taste every inch of him. I slowly glided my tongue up his washboard abs, slowly creeping like a panther in the night. My lips and tongue moved to his nipples. As I sucked his nipples my hand moves to his dick- I need to keep him hard and ready. Before I could climb on top of him and glide my body down to feel all of his sexiness, he quickly grabbed me and flipped me over. I didn't even have an opportunity to protest, he is now eating my pussy from the back. Somehow, we managed to end up in the sixty-nine position. I decide to indulge in his manhood yet again as he uses his tongue to please me in every way possible. *Wait I'm supposed to be controlling this situation.*

As my body responds to each touch, he does the unthinkable; he starts to ease his finger in my ass...pain and pleasure. I try to fight the feeling, but he is too strong, and the feeling is so intense. I'm coming fast and hard, my legs tighten and before I could finish, he moves me to the edge of the bed. Somehow, he manages to end up behind me. As our body moves as one, doggy-style, slow, steady, and in sync. His pace quickens and as my ass pounds his dick I am suddenly screaming his name, within seconds (or so it seemed) he is squirting his semen all over my body, like he is applying lotion on me. The warm liquid just makes me want more.

"Damn." I pant in between breaths.

"Damn is right." He says, "You did are amazing job."

"If you have any left in you, I want you to squirt it in my mouth."

"You are so damn sexy."

"Anything for you babe, I aim to please."

The next morning, I woke with a smile on my face, reaching across the bed to feel for Cedric; I realized he's not there. Sitting up in the bed, looking to the left and then to the right, I see him sitting on my chaise lounge just staring at me.

"Good morning," I say in between stretching and yawning.

"Good morning." He says with a smile in his voice.

"What time is it and how long have you been awake?"

"It's 5:30 am, I haven't been up to long."

"Oh okay, I slept like a baby," I said in between fighting another yawn.

"You are absolutely beautiful," Cedric says slightly above a whisper.

Smiling I say, "Thank you. Can I fix you some breakfast or get you some coffee?"

"No thank, I really need to get going. I have a flight to catch later today."

"Oh." I said, trying to hide the disappointment in my voice, "When are you scheduled to return?"

"I'm not sure, I need to check with my assistant, but I promise I won't make it too long before I see you again."

"Promise?" I questioned with excitement in my voice.

"Sweetheart, I promise."

I slowly removed myself from the bed and walked Cedric downstairs and outside to his car. Before he gets in his car, he gives me a kiss and a hug. Waiting on him to drive off, I turn to walk back into my house, but before I make it to the front door, my nosy, obnoxious neighbor Walter marches across the grass to approach me.

"So, I see you had another overnight guest," he says with hatred and jealousy dripping from his voice.

"And I see you have nothing better to do than to mind my business."

"So, whose husband is it this time?"

"Well we know it wasn't yours."

Walter winces and through clenched teeth he says, "None of them can give you what I can."

Turning around to walk away I say, "Trust me, I am not that desperate."

"WHORE BITCH!" He yells.

"Yo momma, you impotent short bastard," I said while of slamming my front door. *That nerdy mutherfucker has got some nerve, I swear you let a brutha lick your pussy and he swear he owns you.*

"I swear I hate his ass," I say to no one in particular.

As I walked to the kitchen to clean up the mess from the night before, all I can do is smile from the memories. I am so intrigued by Cedric but how could that be possible, I don't even have a clue about him, but I surely will find out more as soon as possible. Deciding to leave the messy kitchen for later, I located my cell phone so I could tell Kelsey about my night, but my call goes straight to voicemail. *Hmm that is so odd, oh well; I will try her again later.* Still feeling refreshed and restless, I decided to go back to bed. Since its Saturday, maybe I will indulge in some shopping after a much-needed nap

Kelsey

Kelsey decided to call it an early day at work, typical Friday fun day. The weather was nice, and she was feeling energetic, so she decided to head to the beach even though DaShawn was at the hotel waiting for her, she decided to change the plans. For a brief moment she just wanted to escape from everything and everyone. Of course, she wanted and needed sexual stimulation right now; she needed to shut down the world more than anything. DaShawn would be pissed, heck he was sure to block Kelsey for a few days but oh well she would worry about that bridge when she is ready to cross it, but in the meantime, she turned on Chrisett Michelle, and pressed the gas pedal to the floor -- leaving it all behind in her rearview mirror.

DaShawn

Waiting in the designated hotel room he shares with Kelsey every week; the fumes of rage are oozing out of his pores. *Who in the fuck does she think she is leaving me here waiting on her?*

"THAT FUCKIN' BITCH!" DaShawn screams to no one in particular. As he sits on the couch-naked; semi-hard; very tipsy; and slightly high, he has a million things going through his head.

DaShawn Jackson - the angry, hurt, neglected half-brother of Barry, yes Barry Simmons - Kelsey's husband. DaShawn has not lived the life as well as Barry did growing up, you see his mother was the side chick and Barry's father never acknowledged DaShawn on birthdays, Christmas, Monday, Tuesday, Wednesday...ever. So needless to say, DaShawn is always finding himself in trouble with the law at least 2 times a year. And rumor in lock-up is Barry is the HNIC (head nigga in charge) at the jail. Barry is living "the good life", a nice position at his job, a beautiful house, a nice car, kids, money, and a wife he cherishes to the utmost. If Barry could put a statue of Kelsey in his office, he surely would. His wife could do no wrong. He hit the jackpot when he met and married Kelsey. DaShawn has heard all the stories about Barry's amazing life so he devised a plan to ruin Barry's life by any means necessary. He could bet the last $3.00 in his pocket that Barry knew about him and his mother - how could he not, he came by the house in the past with his father when he was a kid so when his father died from a "heart attack" more like too much Viagra and a chick young enough to be his granddaughter - but since he was a valued member at Christ on the Rock Church - the appropriate term is a heart attack.

(A few months ago)

It was just a coincidence bumping into Kelsey years ago

leaving the neighborhood Wal-Mart grocery store. DaShawn had just gotten written up-yet again for being inappropriate with a customer so he decided to go outside for some fresh air when he noticed Kelsey sashaying across the parking lot. He remembered seeing her picture in Barry's office and the plan he had to get back at Barry just got a bit easier. He decided to make her a part of the "get back at that MF plan." He started tracking across the parking lot to catch up to her, and without hesitation, bumped into her. Before she could curse him out (because we know how ghetto Kelsey can be) he apologizes to her and throws on the hustle charm, and the rest is history.

Present – day

DaShawn was getting tired of being a joke to everyone, he needed to make changes to his plan, and he needed to do something sooner than later. His original plan was to make Barry pay, but since Kelsey is suddenly taking him for granted as well, now she is being added to the hit list. His mother died a slow painful death and he was not there to say his goodbyes because he was in lock-up from a burglary gone wrong. His mother was his everything and, in his heart, he felt that he failed her - someone has to pay for this, and trust you, they will feel the same pain he and his mother felt.

Stephanie

Waking up refreshed from a much-needed nap, I decided to get my day started by opening up the curtains in the house to let the natural light flow throughout the house. *Today would be a great day to do some retail therapy; I need to call Kelsey to see what she has going on today.* In the process of opening the blinds to the patio door, my mind drifts back to the amazing night I had with Cedric. Stephanie mind drifted back to another time when she had an amazing sexual experience with a man she had just met.

March 2017

Aimlessly walking around the grocery store with no idea of what I wanted or needed and not paying attention to which way I was headed; my shopping cart crashes into his cart.

"Oh man, I am so sorry."

"No, no need to apologize, I wasn't paying attention."
He stammers and avoids my eyes.

"No really, it was my fault," I say as I examine all the
frozen food in his cart. I smile and reply, "So I see you aren't
much of a chef."

"What gave it away, the frozen food or the frozen?" He
laughs.

"I'm Stephanie," as I extend my hand to his.

"Nice to meet you, Stephanie, I am Chad."
Chad was not black nor was he white, hell he had something in
the milk, but it was a good mixture...a mixture that sparked my
curiosity. I did not want this short run-in to end, but I did not
want to seem desperate either.

"Well happy shopping," I say as I sashay off to the next
aisle.

Frustrated with my failed attempt to get his number and
to successfully grocery shop, I decided to ditch the shopping

cart and grab a bottle of wine to drink later. As I approached the register, I quickly notice the long lines. Damn, why are there twelve registers and only two of them are always open, I say under my breath. Wanting to even forget the wine, I noticed Chad in the checkout line, he notices me and smiles, and waves for me to come towards him. With a confused look on my face I mouthed "me?" He nods yes, as I walked towards him; he reaches for the bottle of wine.

"Please add this to my order." He says to the cashier.

"Wait, I can pay for my wine."

"Let a man be a man," Chad says in a strong, bold voice.

"Oh... o-k-a-y." I mentioned as I handed him the bottle.

Feeling a bit weird, I wait for him to pay for his groceries and as we walk to the parking lot with no word from either of us, I grabbed the bottle from his cart, say a quick thank you, and speed-walked to my car. There is something

*about Chad that is sexy and scary all at the same time. As I
unlock my car door, I notice his reflection in my car window,
as soon as I turn around; he grabs me and begins to
passionately kiss me. Not having a chance to think, I quickly
follow his lead. His kiss was everything. As if on cue, the rain
starts to downpour, he releases my face, grabs my hand, and
begins to run to the nearest alley. Not having an opportunity to
protest, I follow him. Once we made it to the alley, I am
suddenly pushed up against the building and he begins to kiss
me again. Chad is exploring my mouth like his life depended on
it. Sweet Jesus, I wanted this man - this stranger. Chad
suddenly turns me around and as I am gripping this brick wall,
in the pouring rain, he lifts my skirt and slides his finger in me.*

"Mmm"

*"Oh shit, you are so wet." Slowly caressing my clit,
without another thought, he inserts two fingers.*

*"WAIT!" I practically yell. Panic is in my voice. Not
listening, he tears my panties off with one hand and he uses his*

forearm from his other hand to hold me in place against the wall. He wrestles with his pants to free his penis. Quickly glancing over my shoulder, I noticed how thick, hard, and ready he is but before I can object, he inserts himself in my vagina.

"NO WAIT, CHAD PLEASE STOP!" I am begging.

Ignoring my plea, he continues to fuck me...in the rain...in the alley... up against the A&P Grocery Store. Granted it was good because it was raw, dirty, and dangerous but this had to stop. As if he was reading my mind, Chad stopped, zipped up his pants, and walked away. He gets to this car, put his soaking wet groceries in his car, get in the driver seat, turns to me (I'm still in the alley-dazed, confused, breathless, and still slightly aroused) blows me a kiss and drives off. What in the fuck just happened? Adjusting my skirt, I sashay back to my car, gently ease into the driver's seat, and hysterically start laughing. What in the fuck just happened? My laugh now turns to tears, tears of hurt, pain, and pleasure.

Sitting in my car, my weave is matted, my clothes are soaked, and my panties are missing, and all the while, my pussy is still pulsating. And with all that all I can do is laugh.

Present Day

The thought of that incident still makes Stephanie blush. *I was such a fool.* Shrugging off the past, I yell for Alexa to play LL Cool J song *Head sprung*, as I danced around the room without a care in the world, I am doing a one-person electric slide, two-stepping, twerking, and dropping it like it was hot. I started laughing at no one and nothing in particular until I was drained.

Little did Stephanie know, as she is dropping it low and spreading it wide, Walter is peaking in the patio door, enjoying the view.

Kelsey

Kelsey could not recall the events from the day before.

She remembered driving towards the beach, but everything afterward is a blur. Reaching for her buzzing cell phone, she declines the call and tossed the phone in the bed next to her. Suddenly noticing Barry's side of the bed had not been slept in she finally opened her eyes to realize she is not in her bed; in fact, she is not even in her house.

What in the devil. Suddenly a man appears from the bathroom, still wet from the shower, a milky white man seemed to have drifted through the fog that is seeping from the bathroom. Not only was he white, but he was milky white, chiseled body-abs for days, piercing blue eyes, and a smirk that send chills down Kelsey's spine.

"Holy shit". She whispered.

"Good morning." Whitey McWhite said.

"Hey," Kelsey mumbled.

"I am surprised you are still here."

"Speaking of here, exactly where is here?" She quizzed.

"Well beautiful, here is my condo."

"And you are?"

"Now I'm really hurt." He says as he smiles and clutches his heart. "My name is Scott, we met at the bar on the beach, umm you had your own party going on at the bar."

"Did I do anything crazy?" She asked as fear creeps in her eyes.

Laughing, Scott replies, "No love, I don't think you did anything crazy. Well unless you consider challenging everyone in the bar to do a shot with you, or trying to do a dance-off to jazz music, and last but not least, trying to climb on top of the bar to twerk is crazy, then I would suggest you never show your face again at the Beach Bum.

"You are lying," Kelsey screams, with the look of terror in her eyes.

"I have the video." He says as he reached for his phone. Pressing the play button, Kelsey throws the cover over her head and fell back onto the pillows.

"I swear, I do not remember what happened. How did I end up here? Wait.... did we have sex? Where are my clothes? Where is my car?" Kelsey is frantically asking question after question.

"Shh, everything is going to be okay." Reaching his hands out to calm Kelsey's frantic state, "I brought you back to my condo after the bartender threatened to call the police. Your clothes are in the dryer, no we did not have sex...well not sex - sex but your pussy is the best I have ever licked, I'm guessing you like strawberries, and your car is still in the parking lot at the bar."

Blushing Kelsey inquires, "Well I guess I should be thanking you, huh?"

"Tasting your strawberry patch was thank you enough," Scott said.

If Kelsey could have turned red, she would have turned "strawberry red". Picking up the pillow behind her, she playfully tossed it towards Scott, but he blocked it with his hand and proceeded to jump on Kelsey, losing his towel in the midst of their playing, Kelsey noticed the nice, thick 8 inches.

"Damn, this is what you are working with and all I did was let you graze the field? Well now that I am sober, and will be sure to remember this moment, let me show you how thankful I am for you rescuing me." Kelsey said with a devilish smile on her face.

Grabbing his dick and pushing him on the pillow, she seductively looks up at him and said, "Relax and let me lick this white chocolate bar."

And that is exactly what Kelsey did. She sucked and licked every inch of Scott, from the balls to the head, and with the mad skills Kelsey has with her mouth (rather it's sucking dick or talking shit) she knows how to shut a man down. Her slow licks turned into hard sucking, as she slobbered the left side, and then the right side she could feel him on the verge of exploding so she puts her mouth on his pink tip and began sucking his dick like she was sucking on a crack pipe.

"OH SHIT!" Scott screams, "Damn love, I might have to marry you!"

Licking the side of her mouth, Kelsey giggled and replied, "If I didn't already have a husband and a boyfriend, I would accept your offer, but I can't and on that note, it's time for me to get back to reality."

Sliding out of the bed, she did a two-step shuffle towards the bathroom, closing the bathroom door Kelsey turned on the shower, sat on the edge of the tub, and cried like she never cried before. The water is helping to drown out her cry but the pain she is feeling is one that no one could ever understand. Her life is spiraling out of control and she has no idea how to get the control back. How is she going to explain not coming home, a home that contains her husband and her children? A home where she should feel safe, peace, and love, instead, it is a home that she constantly avoids.

KNOCK-KNOCK

"Are you okay in there?" Concerned fill's Scott's voice.

"Yes, one second."

Quickly jumping in and out of the shower for the sake of getting wet, she turns off the water, dried her tears and her barely wet body, and exits the bathroom.

"I made you some coffee, it's in the kitchen and your clothes should be ready any second," Scott mentioned.

"Thank you, and for the record, this is not something I normally do."

Slowly approaching her, he reaches out to hug Kelsey, but before she can protest the dryer buzzed. Feeling the awkward tension, Shawn says, "Saved by the buzzer."

Returning to the room with her clothes and a cup of

coffee in his hand, he gives them both to her and sits in the chair next to the bed. Without saying a word or making eye contact, Kelsey quickly puts her clothes on so she could prepare herself to leave Scott's place and head home. Once she was ready, Scott grabbed his keys so he could take her back to her car. As they walked outside, the warm beach air helped to warm Kelsey's spirit. Walking in silence until they reached the car, Scott pulled her into a hug and whispered in her ear letting her know that everything was going to be okay.

"Kelsey, please know this is a no-judgment zone. I am here if you ever need to talk or getaway. Here is my card; my cell phone number is listed on it as well."

"Thank you, Scott, I will keep you in mind."

Without any further discussion he drops her off to her car, kisses her cheek, and reminds her that he is just a phone call away. Kelsey got in her car and retrieved her phone; she noticed all of the missed calls, voice messages, and text messages from Barry and DaShawn; she took a deep breath and calls Stephanie.

"Hey, sis, where in the hell have you been?" I questioned.

"I need to talk, please let me come over... sis I need you." Kelsey pleaded with me.

"Girl I have the wine ready, see you soon."

Stephanie

Kelsey did not sound like herself when she called me.

As I prepare for Kelsey's arrival, I pulled out the wine glasses, and made a fruit tray - because presentation is everything and put on some smooth jazz music to help ease the mood. I still had time to run upstairs and change clothes, so I decided to throw on my Fendi sundress and some fuzzy socks. Suddenly, I hear my doorbell constantly ringing and someone was banging on my front door. Approaching the front door, I could see Kelsey, but it was not the bubbly Kelsey I was accustomed to; this Kelsey was sad and somber. As I quickly opened the door, Kelsey fell into my arms and began to cry. I am shocked and confused but at the very moment all I could do was hold her as she cried. I ushered her to the sofa and grabbed the cocktail napkin off the table so she could dry her eyes.

"Baby please talk to me, who hurt my sister?"

"No one, I'm just sad today." She lied, "Today is the anniversary of my deceased sister." Another lie.

Kelsey did not want Stephanie to know how fucked up her life is right now. It took Kelsey a few minutes to compose herself. Afterward she and Stephanie laughed, talked, drank wine, and enjoyed the day. Even though Stephanie wanted to do some retail therapy, having girl time was just as good. She had a chance to tell Kelsey all about Cedric and about the crazy run-in with Walter the Weirdo. It was fun and refreshing catching up like old times. Kelsey was enjoying the quality time she was sharing with Stephanie, but in reality, she was buying time to avoid going home to face Barry. She would have to face the music sooner than later.

Kelsey

Kelsey and Stephanie parted ways, she can't recall the last she enjoyed just being, not having to be-do-or-think. Now it was time to go home and face Barry, and eventually DaShawn. As she was trying to piece together the events from the night before she can't figure out how she ended up in the bed of a stranger. Pulling up in her driveway she put her car in park, said a silent prayer, and stepped out of her car. Slowly walking up the path to the front door she takes a deep breath, but when she inserted the key in the lock nothing happens.

"What the fuck!" Kelsey yells as she bangs on the front door. In mid - pound the front door flew open, and there stood Barry with hatred in his eyes.

"WHAT!" He yells.

Rolling her eyes, Kelsey tries to slide by him and walk in the house, but Barry quickly blocked her attempt. Feeling exhausted and defeated, she steps back and asks, "What is this all about Barry?"

"Where in the hell have you been over the last few days?"

"It wasn't a few days - it was a day and a half." She smirks.

"So, you want to challenge me right now?"

Sigh.

"No, I want a hot shower and a Tylenol PM right now."

"Kelsey, I am on the verge of divorcing you and you don't seem to care. What is really going on with you? Where have you been? Is there someone else in your life?"

Not caring to answer all of Barry's questions - all she wants is access to her house and her bed.

"Look, babe, I'm really tired. I just want to lie down for a few hours and then I promise I will tell you whatever it is you want and need to know. Now, please let me in the house."

Kelsey said as she lets her guard down with Barry. Without another thought, he leaned in and kissed Kelsey and stepped aside to let her in the house.

What a weak man. She thought as she walked into the house. Taking a few steps, Kelsey stops, turns around and punches Barry in his left eye.

"Don't ever try that shit again, change the locks back to the old ones, and don't wake me up from my damn nap."

Feeling defeated once again, Barry nods as he stands there holding his hands over his left eye. His father has to be rolling over in his grave knowing his son is a "yes man" and has no control in his own house. Barry has to think of another plan to get Kelsey's attention because obviously this one failed.

Stephanie

Things have been going really great in my life. Work has been busy and non-stop, my friendship with Kelsey still has its ups and downs but it was mainly on Kelsey's part because she obviously had a lot going on in her personal life and whenever she is ready to talk about it, I will be ready to talk about it, I will make myself available. Cedric and I talk on a regular basis. We practically know everything about each other. If we aren't on the phone talking, we are texting all day in between meetings, eating, and sleeping. We have really gotten to know so much about either other over the last few months, and of course we have been flying back and forth visiting each other. Since Cedric travels a lot, I always enjoy mini vacations meeting him at his next destination. Meeting him at various places helps to relieve our stress and tension from our everyday living. If I did not know any better, I would have thought I was falling in love with him. How could this be happening - heck I have only known him for a few months, but whatever, I am happy.

A feeling of happiness was something that Stephanie was feeling, and it was a weird feeling because that does not exist very long in Stephanie's life. The idea of being married again and waking up next to such an amazing guy is something she could really see in her future. They made plans for him to fly in and spend a non-work-related weekend together and she could not wait to see him, touch him, and most importantly feel each and every part of him. In her thoughts of making plans with Cedric for the weekend, her cell phone rang, from a blocked number. "Hello?"

CLICK

Hmm that was weird. She thought.

Reverting her mind back to Cedric and trying to decide when she will tell him all about her past life, her mother, her ex-husband, her deceased twins, and how she has trust issues.

Ring… ring…

"Hello?"

CLICK

"Seriously, the next time I am not even going to answer the damn phone," Stephanie mentioned in frustration.

Ring… Ring… Ding… Dong, Stephanie jumped; her cell phone and doorbell went off simultaneously.

"SHIT! I'm losing it."

Refusing to answer her cell phone, she decided to answer the front door. Greeting her at the front door was a delivery man, holding a beautiful bouquet of rainbow roses.

"I have a delivery for Stephanie Xavier." The delivery guy says as he hands her the oversized vase.

"Oh wow!" Stephanie mentioned with too much excitement in her voice. "That would be me!" Reaching for the vase and inhaling the overwhelming scent of fresh-cut flowers. "Do I need to sign anything?"

"No ma'am, enjoy your bouquet." He says.

"Thank you, I will."

As she struggles to close the door, there goes Walter standing on his porch glaring at her. Feeling uneasy, Stephanie quickly closes her door. Hmm, no card, but they have to be from Cedric. I will be sure to thank him when we speak tonight.

Justin

Justin's life has been up and down since Stephanie walked...more like ran out of his life. He could not get it together, when his love life was working, his career wasn't and vice versa. He has changed from the abusive person he was when he was married to Stephanie - well he wasn't as abusive like he used to be, but he has no problem reminding the women in his life who the man is in the relationship.

He has asked God to forgive him so that he could forgive himself, but for him to really move forward, he needed to ask Stephanie to forgive him for all of the awful things he has done to her, but he needed to find her. All of the leads he had always turned out to be dead ends. He was not sure if she was still carrying his last name, if she still lived in the same state, or if she was even alive. Tired of the constant disappointment, he decided to take the last bit of money from his savings account and hire a private investigator to locate Stephanie; after all, she was the love of his life and he was ready to apologize and win her back so that he could give her the life he promised her over 15 years ago.

I will find you and make you mine again, by any means necessary.

Cedric

Cedric has been putting fires out and saving failing companies left and right for the last few months. He is ready for a Netflix weekend with Stephanie. Sure, they talk and text all the time, but he wanted her scent, her flesh, her long chocolate legs wrapped around his body. Stephanie was a breath of fresh air compared to some of the psycho's he has dealt with in the past. They were always pressuring him to settle down and get married, while he enjoyed the thought of not having to be committed to anyone. He tried the marriage thing-four times to be exact, and they always failed. Women tend to be nice, sweet, and gentle when you first meet them. When you marry them- they suddenly become possessive and clingy. He vowed to be married-he did not vow to be on lockdown. After the last wife, he swore off all women who wanted to be married, exclusive, and committed. Stephanie was the complete opposite-so he thought. Putting the final pieces of clothes in his suitcase he reached for his vibrating phone and smiles when Stephanie's phone number showed on the screen.

"Hey, beautiful."

"Hey, cutie pie." She purred.

"I was just thinking about you. I can't wait to see you this weekend."

"Neither can I," she mentioned. "I was calling to thank you for the beautiful flowers."

"What flowers?" Cedric asked. "I didn't send you any flowers. Is there something you want to tell me?" Concern and jealousy take over his mind.

Laughing Stephanie replies, "Umm okay, sure I will play along."

"I am not laughing or playing," Cedric replies but before he could address the issue any further his work cell phone rang. "Hey this is a client calling; we will finish this conversation later."

"Okay sure and again thank you, the flowers are beautiful," Stephanie says before she hung up the phone.

Cedric answered his cell phone and spoke to his client for over 30 minutes but the entire time his mind was on Stephanie and the flowers some other guy apparently sent her. Why was he concerned or even cared, he is not nor will he be a jealous man, but for some reason, he was definitely feeling some type of way. Could it be he was starting to have feelings for Stephanie? It couldn't be-it's only been a few months and yes, he cared for her, but this jealous feeling was something he was not used to feeling, could it be possible he was falling in love? Shaking his head, he tells himself, naw bruh, it's not possible.

Kelsey

Since the run-in with Barry a few months ago, Kelsey decided to stay on the right path before her cover was blown. Her midnight and overnight stays have ceased, and she is now home at a reasonable time each night. DaShawn has now been upgraded to lunch dates and quickies rather than late-night dinner and desserts. Everyone is back in their opposing corners and all is well in Kelsey's life or, so she is trying to convince herself. Ever since she met Scott, she seems to be fascinated with him. She would have never thought to be with a white man, but Scott had a soft caring side to him that Kelsey did not realize was an important factor that needed to be added to the equation. Barry was the protector and cared about her well-being, but that was his job as a husband and father so technically that did not count. DaShawn cared about pleasing her in the bedroom but what did she really know about him -

absolutely nothing. She seemed like the one who was taking care of him... financially and emotionally. Heck, physical care was something she could do for herself, as we already know and can attest to, but Scott took the time to genuinely care that she was okay. The "no judgment zone" as he called it when they last saw each other.

I wonder if I should give him a call...will he even remember me?

"There is only one way to find out," she says to no one in particular.

"Hello?" Scott answered the phone in a questioning tone.

"Umm, hi," Kelsey struggled to get her words out - she was truly nervous. A rare feeling to Kelsey.

"Hi. How can I help you?"

"Hi – oh, I already said that, I'm sorry," she rambles, "Umm this is Kelsey, you may not remember me, but umm..."

"Oh, my strawberry patch." He says in a light chuckle.

Blushing Kelsey replies, "Yes, it is. How have you been? Did I catch you at an okay time? Do you want me to call you back?" Nervousness sets in and she could not stop rambling.

"Slow down Love, everything is good. How have you been?" He asked. "I have been thinking a lot about you. I am really glad you called. Are you okay?" Scott seemed to have the same nervous rambling as Kelsey.

"I don't want to disturb you, but I wanted to once again thank you for rescuing me."

"Honestly, it was my pleasure; I would do it again if I had to." He mentioned with a bit of hesitation in his voice. "So how have you been…I mean really been?"

"I'm okay, trying to behave myself and stay out of trouble."

"That's good to hear. I was so worried about you after you left, I realized I did not get your phone number, so I am so glad you called me." Worry and concern showed on his face and filled his voice.

"I wanted to thank you for being there for me, so I was calling to see if I could take you out to show you my appreciation."

"That would be refreshing; I would love to see you again. Are you free this evening?"

"Absolutely, let's plan on meeting around 6. I usually frequent this hot spot called the Red Rooster, have you heard of it?" She asked.

"Aww man, I have been dying to visit that bar. I heard nice things about it. Consider it a date. I will see you at 6."

"Consider it a date - see you then," Kelsey says as she ends the call.

A date. Far from it. I am simply buying him a drink to thank him for saving me and that will be the end of Scott.

So, she hopes.

Stephanie

The week was a blur, in between working and preparing herself and her house for Cedric's upcoming visit, she was determined to let nothing ruin her weekend. The blocked calls were still coming at odd times of the day and night, but Stephanie could care less because this weekend her phone will be turned off. So, whoever it was would have to find someone else to annoy for the next few days. The house was ready, the fridge was stocked with all his favorite food and drinks and Stephanie had been waxed, plucked, pulled, and pampered in anticipation for Cedric's visit. While running errands on her extended lunch break, she made a trip to the outlet mall to pick up a few needed body scents from Bath & Body Works. As she is aimlessly wandering from store to store, she suddenly gets a sick uneasy feeling, the feeling of evil. The last time she felt this was when she left Justin.

This cannot be happening. I am sure he moved on with his life and could care less about me. Get it together Steph.

Still feeling unsettled, no matter how much she tried to convince herself she was being silly, she decided to get her items and head back to the office where it was safe. *No worries, Cedric will be here to protect me this weekend, and with everything that is needed for this weekend, there is no reason to leave the house.*

Justin

As I'm walking around the outlet mall, I could have sworn I saw Stephanie, but it couldn't be her-this female was bold, confident, and drop-dead gorgeous. Don't get me wrong my bae was absolutely beautiful but this lady was making my dick hard, just watching her was invigorating.

Justin was so mesmerized by this female, that he did not realize he was following Stephanie. His body and mind were bombarded with a flow of emotions. He wanted to rush up to her and give her the biggest hug, but he had to refrain because of their past and his history of violence. How could he have been this close to her all these years and never ran into her before now? Was this another sign from God that after all these years their relationship could possibly re-kindle, but on a better non-abusive, more mature level? He completed his court-ordered anger management sessions, he only drinks on special occasions, and he has not had to hit anyone…well not this month, so he is doing really well, and he is ready to rekindle the relationship with his first and only love. Coming back to reality, Justin did not realize he was standing in the store alone. He needed answers right away.

"Hello," Justin speaks into his cell phone.

"Yes." The other person on the other end replies.

"What's the status of my case?"

"I have some information for you; meet me at my office in one hour."

Disconnecting the call, Justin makes a b-line to his car. Finally, he is going to get information from the private investigator he has been seeking.

Stephanie

Cedric called to let me know he just picked up his car from the rental agency and should be at my house in about twenty minutes, so I am running around lighting candles, putting the steaks on the Foreman, and putting all of the final touches on everything else that will contribute to an amazing night and weekend. Losing track of time, my mind shifts back to Cedric… *He should have been here by now.* I called his cell phone, but it went to voicemail. *WTF?* Walking to the front door, I hear voices but before I open the door, I had to tie the belt on my robe because I am very naked underneath. Opening the door Cedric stops talking and looks at me and smiles.

"Hey." He said.

"Hey," I said with a confused look on my face. "Who are you talking to?"

"Your neighbor Walter, he was kind enough to ask if I needed help with my bags."

"Hello Stephanie," Walter says with a sly grin on his face.

Ignoring him, I stretched my hand out and pulled Cedric into the house and slammed my front door.

"What was that about?" Cedric inquired.

"That guy is creepy."

"He seems pretty cool; in fact, he was about to give me the dirt on you." He chuckled.

"Dirt? That weirdo better tread lightly." I hiss.

"Hmm, okay. So, he does know things?"

"I know this…" I said as I stepped towards him, untied my robe, and passionately kissed him.

"Wow." He replies. "Maybe I need to go outside again."

Laughing at his silly response, I pulled him into the living room and moved in for another kiss.

The passion between the two of them was not an issue. As Cedric explores every inch of her naked body, she is welcoming every gesture he is providing. Moving to the bedroom was not an option; the fire was burning right then and there. No longer able to control his urges, Cedric quickly unbuckles his pants, his dick was hard and ready, holding her with one hand, he used the other hand to free himself. The tip of his penis was already wet, swollen, and hot. He needed to be inside of her warm, wet cave... right this instant. Stephanie moaned with anticipation. She fantasized about this moment all week and finally it was happening. Cedric was there in the flesh.

As my robe fell to the floor, I turned around so Cedric could enter my throbbing pussy from the back. Forcefully inserting his dick inside of me, I gasp and held on to the couch with all of my might. He was pounding me - it was rough and hard but sexy as fuck. Suddenly, I see a flash - not sure if it's from the candle, the TV, or something in my mind. I continued to meet Cedric's force pound for pound. There it goes again. *What in the hell?* And then I see it... I see him...Walter is looking at us. *So, this bitch wants to look, well I will give him something to look at...*I reached down and inserted my fingers into my pussy and slowly, seductively licked my fingers and as I am tasting myself, I am looking Walter in his eyes. *Now enjoy that you freak.* Meanwhile, I continue to moan and scream louder and louder. I motion Cedric to the couch, he follows, and we continue to fuck. He is sucking and biting my nipples and I am pulling him into me more and more. I need every inch of him. My legs are wrapped around his waist, my ass is lifted in both of his hands, and in the midst of all of that, I still manage to slip my hands in between us and feel his shaft. I am massaging his balls and the look on his face intensifies. I reached for my pussy again and began inserting my fingers, this time; I let him taste each finger.

"Mmm." He moans.

"I'm about to cum," I whisper.

"Not yet." He demands.

Releasing me he now lowers his head between my legs, and whisper, "Cum in my mouth."

Pulling his head deep into my walls I feel his tongue licking and sucking and exploring every inch of me, and before he could sink his tongue any deeper in me, I exploded. Moaning and screaming his name, he continued to lick and suck and I cum again. I see another flash- *this bitch won't go away.* In the midst of me trying to cum again, I shift my head to the right, and Walter is on my patio stroking his dick as he watches us... and Cedric is none the wiser. I need to get control of both situations right now. I pushed Cedric's head from in between my legs, I command him to switch places. It's my turn to taste him. I take his wet, sticky from all of my juices, hard dick into my mouth. As I look into his eyes, I see the pleasure and the urge he is trying not to cum, but I am winning this battle. I suck, lick, and play with his balls and within seconds I am swallowing all of him. His cum is hot, thick, and delicious.

As Cedric works to catch his breath, Stephanie strokes his chest and turns to look outside but Walter is gone. *That will teach him-crazy bastard.*

"Damn babe, that shit was intense. I need to make you wait more often." Cedric says in between breaths.

"This is just the beginning of an amazing weekend." She smirks.

"I look forward to round two, but first I need to replenish my energy. What's for dinner?"

"I guess I will feed you dinner, but eat fast because round two is dessert, and that will be me!"

Cedric

Cedric was exhausted, famished, and happy to be in Stephanie's presence. She was definitely the total package... sexy, smart, educated, and beautiful; she can cook, she can hold her own and was not clingy. He could get used to this type of a relationship. But who was Stephanie Xavier? Since he thought she was such an amazing woman, he wondered why she was single, what dirt did her neighbor really have on her, and who sent her those damn roses. He saw them when she escorted him into the living room. He couldn't avoid the huge flower arrangements, sitting on the table toying with his emotions. Looking at them was a total slap in his face so he thought. That is why he tried to hurt her with every thrust he did, he wanted her to feel pain while he took pleasure in hurting her...just like the sight of those flowers were hurting him.

Every time I opened my eyes and saw those fucking flowers, I felt the need to fuck her harder and harder. I will make her pay for every stem in that damn vase. Who in the fuck sent them to her? Well if she is giving her pussy to someone else-they will know that I was here. I am branding my name all over her shit this weekend and trust me I will hook up with Walther again before it's too late.

Kelsey

Kelsey could not wait to meet Scott after work. In fact, she was a little too excited all day long. She had been telling herself it's just drinks and an appreciation gesture, no more…no less, so why was she so nervous?

Calm down, damn it's just a drink. Kelsey arrived at the Red Rooster a few minutes early so she could get a drink to help calm her nerves.

"Hi Donna. How have you been?"

"Hey pretty lady, how is it going?"

"Living the dream!" She said in a sarcastic tone. "I am meeting someone here, but I think I need a drink before he arrives. Can I get the usual?"

"Okay," Donna replied with a concerned look on her face.

Picking up on Donna's concern, Kelsey quickly replies, "Oh no girl, everything is good - this is a business meeting."

"Okay, I was wondering if I needed to call for back-up," Donna chuckles.

"As if security could get here before I beat his ass. You know I don't play!"

They both laughed as Donna went to retrieve Kelsey's drink. Wanting to calm her nerves, she busied herself by strolling through her phone; she was so busy that she did not notice DaShawn sitting in the corner. He watched her for a few minutes, trying to decide if he should go over and sit with her but before he could move, Scott walked up to her table, gave her a hug and a kiss on her cheek and slid in the booth next to Kelsey.

"Hey love." He says with a gleam in his eyes.

"Hi Scott, you are a little early."

"I couldn't wait to see you."

Holding up her hand to stop him, Kelsey said, "I don't want you to get the wrong idea as to why I invited you out for drinks. I wanted…"

Grabbing her hands, and holding them much longer than necessary, he questioned, "So am I to assume you really did not want to see me? You don't fantasize about me as much as I fantasize about you? Tell me I am wrong."

Not removing his hands, she released a long breath, "Scott, whatever happened a few weeks ago, cannot happen again."

"Why not?"

Before she could respond, her cell phone vibrated in her purse. Kelsey quickly sent the call to voicemail.

"Because we…" Her phone vibrates again; she quickly shuts the phone off. She will deal with DaShawn later. "As I was saying, because my life is very difficult right now, and I don't need or want to bring you into this mess… my mess."

"I'm a big boy; I can handle anything you throw at me." He chuckles.

"Trust me, you can't handle this."

"Give me a chance. Let me take all of your pain away."

Shit.

"Let's get out of here. I want to taste you again."

Shit.

"Scott." She tried to protest.

He gently kissed her hand, and slid out of the booth, he placed a hundred-dollar bill on the table and ushered her out of the bar, no questions asked.

DaShawn

DaShawn decided to visit the Red Rooster since he kept hearing nice things about the place. As he sat in the corner nursing his watered-down drink, contemplating his next move with making Kelsey and Barry pay for his downfalls, he noticed a beautiful, voluptuous woman sashay in the bar. She looked familiar but he couldn't get a good look at her because the hostess was blocking this chic's face, but her body was speaking volumes. His dick jumped a little. He hasn't been with Kelsey in a few days, all of a sudden, she wanted to be a good wife and change the rules of the game. He was pissed at her, but he was more pissed at himself for letting her get the upper hand, but that was not his concern right this second - he wanted to approach the banging body chick that was too friendly with the hostess. He wanted to buy her a few drinks, get her tipsy, and take her home and fuck her until the sun came up. As the hostess turns to leave, he noticed her... Kelsey, sitting there looking amazing as ever.

What in the fuck? So, this is why I haven't heard from her all day.

As he stood to approach her, some white guy takes a seat in the spot he should have been sitting in.

What is really going on?

DaShawn reaches for his phone to call her and watched as she kept sending his calls to voicemail.

This bitch! He called her again and watched her once again reject him. Beads of sweat start to form on his forehead. *I am going to fuck this bitch up when I get my hands on her...NOW I AM TAKING CHARGE AGAIN-GAME ON –THIS BITCH IS DEAD!*

Stephanie

The weekend with Cedric was everything she dreamt of and more. They laughed, talked, cuddled, had sex, made love, fucked, and fucked some more. She was in a blissful place in her mind and her heart. Her phone was turned off the entire weekend, so she did not have to concern herself with the annoying phone calls. Her pesky neighbor stayed out of her way, Kelsey was out doing who knows what with who knows who, but it was all great regardless. She could mentally say this past weekend has been one for the books. Cedric tried to inquire more about her past, but she still was not ready to share, so to keep him happy, she gave just enough information. She personally did not believe Cedric was prepared to accept her based on her past. However, she made a promise to herself to come clean the next time they are together, but for now she was driving to work with a smile on her face. That is until her cell phone started ringing again from a blocked number.

"Hello?" No response. "Hello! Who in the fuck is this?"
The caller hangs up.

*So much for having a great day, I swear nobody better fuck
with me today, guns locked and loaded.* I was so pissed from
the idiot who has decided to play on my phone; I didn't even
notice the police car behind me until he almost cut me off, *this
bitch.* I pulled over with a straight-up attitude. He comes up to
the car and I make his ass wait, so he decides to tap on the
window.

"Yes, how can I help you?"

"Do you know why I pulled you over?" He asked.

As I rolled my eyes, I replied "Umm, no I sure don't,
you care to share?"

He smirks and says, "You ran a yellow light back there."

WTF? It took him longer to walk to my car with this shit, okay S.E.X., let him have it.

Sad face, puppy dog eyes, "What light, are you sure it was yellow?"

Now he smiles, hmm he is kinda cute. It is true, there is nothing like a man in uniform. *Nice body, kinda look like that rapper TI. I've never been with a police officer, hmm.* According to his badge, his name is Jonathan Miller.

I licked my lips and ask again, "umm are you sure the light was yellow?"

And his smart ass replied, "Ma'am just because you can't tell your colors, doesn't mean I can't either."

Did this bitch just get smart with me?

As I prepared to tell his short ass off, he smiled and said, "I am just messing with you, but yes it was yellow."

"Oh, okay, so I get off with a warning today-right?"

"Sorry, no warning today, I need your license, registration, and proof of insurance please." As I cursed, and rolled my eyes, I thought to myself, his little ass apparently like white girls. I gave him the information he requested, and as he is in the process of writing me a ticket, my phone rings again- unknown number, *fuck it- voicemail you go*!

Now, he decided to be nosey, and said, "You could have answered your phone call."

Well, now that I am getting a ticket, this bitch has no sympathy from me, "Umm thank you for giving me permission to answer the phone I seem to pay for every month."

He stops writing and puts that damn smirk on his face again, "There is no need to get rude, I was only stating a fact."

"Well fact this, when you are ready to pay the bill associated with this phone number then you can have all the say you want to, but until then, write the damn ticket so I can go." *Oh shit, did I say that out loud?*

Now he proceeded to lean over and looks me dead in my eyes and said, "Smart mouth, hmm, I like that." "What else can you do with that smart mouth?"

Is this bitch flirting with me, in the process of writing me a ticket? "How about you give me your number and I will gladly show you what I can do with this mouth."

"Okay, Mrs. Xavier."

"It's Miss."

"Even better, well here is my phone number and a warning, have a good day, and be safe out there"

"Thank you, Mr. Officer, I will be sure to have a good day, if you promise me, I will have a better night."

"Well Miss, that can be arranged, I get off at 5, make sure you use the number." He said with a smirk on his face. Hmph momma ain't raised no fool, I will be sure to give him a call tonight.

Well looks like my day is getting back to being good. Now I just need to get through these next 8 hours, so I can see how well Officer Jonathan knows how to use his handcuffs.

As I walk into the office, Kelsey is waiting for me at my desk, *oh lord not before I had my coffee... shit.*

"Where in the hell have you been?" She asked.

"Good morning to you too," I replied, with a neck and eye roll.

"Bitch, your ass is late. How much dick did you get over the weekend?"

"Umm a woman never kisses and tells," I replied.

"Women, don't whores do, so spill it."

Damn, I hate this bitch. "My weekend was fantastic, thank you for asking. What did you do this weekend?

"Don't mind my damn business. "Kelsey says, a little too quickly.

Really, I hate this bitch." Whatever, man. Cedric and I spent all weekend talking and getting to know each other."

"So, that is girl code for you fucked him up and down."

"Why would you say that?" I gasp.

"Umm hello, ring, ring, you haven't met a dick you have ever turn down." She states as she is cracking up.

Sigh, I need new friends. "Well, maybe you are right. The weekend was one to remember, but girl I have to tell you about the police officer who just pulled me over. We will talk after this meeting.

Kelsey

Since her last "hoe-down" with Scott, Kelsey is overwhelmed with life. The idea of adding another name to the roster was making her head spin and her pussy moist; thinking about bringing all three of them together would be the ultimate fantasy. She planned to meet Scott, have a drink or two, and bid him farewell, but if only it was that easy. Scott had a sexiness about him that made Kelsey desire more from him. After leaving the bar, Kelsey followed him back to his house and allowed him the opportunity to help her feel like a woman. Scott played with the parts of her body that had been ignored for years... her mind. He catered to her every need - he ran her a hot bubble bath with lavender, he poured her a tall glass of wine, he lit candles, played jazz softly in the background and he bathed her from head to toe. What else could someone ask for... as much as she silently prayed that this could be her life, she knew this could never be, in fact this could not go beyond tonight.

"Love, you are so beautiful. Why won't you allow me the chance to show you how much I can take all of your pain away?" Scott inquired.

"Because life is not that simple, or rather, my life if not that simple," Kelsey replied, with sadness dripping from her voice.

"But if you allow me the chance, I can make your life simple. Just trust me."

Laughing, she replied, "The last man who told me to trust him, ended up with a black eye."

"I don't understand."

"Never mind, I am sure you did not ask me here to talk."

"Actually, I did. I just want to hear you, see you, hold you, and as I keep reminding you, I just want to take care of you."

"I'm sorry; I can't allow you to do any of those things."

Rising out of the tub, Kelsey grabs a towel off of the rack, and rushes to the bedroom to retrieve her clothes. As she is attempting to get dressed, Scott approaches her and gives her the best hug she can ever recall receiving. Without another word, Kelsey relaxes and lets Scott do the one thing he has been asking for; she let him take care of her. He kissed her, he caressed her, and he held her in his arms until she slowly drifted to sleep.

Justin

Justin felt like his drive to the P.I.'s office took forever when in actuality, it was only thirty minutes. He could not contain his excitement as he rushed into the office.

"I am here to see Mr. King."

"Do you have an appointment?" The woman at the front desk questioned.

"No, but he is expecting me. My name is Justin Xavier."

"One moment, please take a seat and I will let him know you are here."

Justin walked back to the waiting area, but he was too excited to sit down. He wanted answers.

"Mr. Xavier, Mr. King will see you now."

Justin practically ran to his office. When he got to the office, the door was ajar, and Mr. King was sitting at his desk flipping through papers. Justin quickly tapped on the door. Mr. King rose from his desk to shake his hand.

"Thank you for coming in so quickly." Mr. King said.

"It was my pleasure. I'm excited to hear what you found out." Justin mentioned through a wide grin.

"Well according to my research, Ms. Xavier…"

"Mrs." Justin corrects Mr. King.

Wrinkling his forehead, Mr. King tries to continue, "Ms. Xavier seems to be doing really well for herself."

"So, my wife still lives here?"

"Your ex-wife… Mr. Xavier, she is your ex-wife."

"Not in my eyes, she will always be my wife," Justin said, as he tried to control his temper.

"Umm sir, are we going to have an issue, because according to the State of South Carolina, the two of you are divorced." Mr. King said sternly.

Trying not to lose his cool, Justin sits back in his chair and slowly started counting to ten in his head.

"No! No, problem at all. My apologies please continue."

Feeling a little uneasy because Mr. King has seen a lot of crazy stuff in his time, he decided to proceed with caution.

"Ok, she is doing well; she lives in a well-kept neighborhood, has a nice job, and seems to be enjoying life." Mr. King says as he closes the file folder.

"That's all?" Justin questioned.

"Yes, what else would you like to know? You paid me $500 and I gave you $500 worth of answers."

"Well how much more do I need to pay to get an address, pictures, or at least a phone number?" Justin questions while trying to maintain his frustration.

"It's going to cost you at least $5,000 for more detailed information."

"Where am I supposed to get that kind of money?"

"Sir, I am not sure, but I am only stating the facts and informing you of my fees."

Frustration and heat rose inside of Justin, "Thank you; I will see what I can work out. I will be in touch soon."

Rising from his chair, Justin reached out to shake Mr. King's hand. Leaving the office, Justin felt like he had just been hit by a dump truck. *I have to find a way to get this money. Stephanie is so close, and I know once she sees me, we will get back together...I will figure it out. Maybe my new girlfriend can loan me some money.*

DaShawn

DaShawn was pissed beyond pissed with the way things have been going with Kelsey. She was practically slipping through his fingers. He was totally losing control and that was not a part of his plan. Now it was time to get dirty and dangerous. He knew the only way to make the wall fall was by removing brick by brick and that's exactly what he will do... his mother always told him "get them before they get you"... "it is always best to be the hunter rather than the prey" and now Kelsey and Barry are both moving targets."

Don't worry mom, I will make their asses pay for everything. You will be so proud of me. If I have never done right by you, now is the time mom...I promise they will know who I am-who we are when I am done with both of them.

Picking up the phone he first does a Google search for a local florist shop. Finding one close to Kelsey's home, he decided to order two dozen of her favorite flowers... yellow roses, with a card that read - Thank you for last night, you were worth the wait. With a sinister grin on his face, he would like to see the look on both of their faces when the flowers would be delivered to their home. Hmm, there is a way he could actually see the look on their face, he could deliver the flowers himself. He knew for a fact that Kelsey was at work and today was Barry's day off. EPIC, he would change the plans. If she won't come to the mountain - the mountain will come to her.

Later that day

DaShawn picked up the flowers from the florist shop and happily drove to Kelsey's house to make the delivery. He was tickled and giddy with the idea. Pulling up, he hopped out of his car and skipped up the walkway as he made his way to the front door. He couldn't decide if he wanted to ring the bell or knock on the door - he decided to do both.

"Hi, can I help you?" Barry questioned.   "I have a

delivery for Mrs. Kelsey Simmons." DaShawn practically sings.

"I can take them," Barry mentioned with a bit of hesitation in his voice.

"Well she must be a special lady. What's the occasion?"

"Yes, she is. I am kinda wondering what the occasion is myself."

"Well, take care and be blessed my brother."

"Yeah okay," Barry replied as he is looking for a card and trying to close the front door.

As soon as DaShawn pulls out of the driveway, he retrieves his phone to give Kelsey a call. After three rings the call goes to voicemail.

Deshawn did not know who to be more pissed at; Barry for not recognizing him or Kelsey for avoiding him.

In frustration, DaShawn tossed his phone on the passenger seat and sped away.

Kelsey

Kelsey's day had been filled with meetings, deadlines, and needy people. All she wanted to do was float away to a blissful place in her mind. Between work foolishness, her cell phone was no better. She had missed calls from the treacherous three and in all honesty, she was over 2 out of the 3. She wanted to be free, left alone, and at peace. She decided to send all of them the same text message: thinking about you. *See...simple... now everyone can be happy for a few minutes.* But before she could put her phone down, her phone chirps signaling a text message, and then another chirp, and a third chirp.

Damn

Hubby: We need to talk, come home straight after work.

Boy toy: Who dis? (LOL), yeah, I bet you miss me.

White Chocolate: Aww love, you are always on my mind.

Reading the messages, her mind starts to wonder, what is really going on with these 2.

I am so tired of this shit! Okay 2 out of 3… I will play your silly game.

Jonathan

Jonathan was a deputy sheriff for the local county, and he loved his job. The idea of having power and control over people was a turn on for him. Jonathan was an asshole and that thought was an even bigger turn on. He needed to hurry and find his next sex victim so he could release some of his pent-up tension. His sexual appetite was massive, and he still has not found that one woman who could match him toe to toe with his sexual appetite and experiments and using his toys for pleasure.

After giving the ticket to Stephanie, he prayed she would call him. She had the mouth…the attitude...and the need to be put her in her place. If she called, he would invite her over for dinner, conversation, and hopefully a bit of rough sex, but he would have trodden lightly with her because he did not want to scare her off. He needed to release, he was tired of watching porn, he needed flesh, and if he did not get some hot, wet pussy soon he was not going to be responsible for his actions. Jonathan was so deep in thought; he did not realize his cell phone was ringing. Snapping out of his thoughts he reached for his cell phone but frowned because he did not recognize the phone number.

"Hello."

"Hi Jonathan, this is Stephanie, the lady you pulled over this morning."

Smiling he replied, "Oh yes, Ms. Smart Mouth, I did not think you would call. What's up?"

"Nothing much, I am about to leave the office and wanted to know if you would like to go out for a drink." Stephanie inquired.

"That sounds nice and tempting; but how about you come to my place instead. I could cook you dinner and I have an array of assorted wines, I am sure you will find one you might like." Jonathan mentioned, more like insisted she accept his offer.

"Umm your place?" Stephanie questioned.

"Yes, I insist. What... you don't trust me" I'm a police officer - correction, a fine black police officer. I am paid to keep people safe." He chuckled.

"Well, now that you put it like that...well specifically the fine part, how could I refuse?"

"I like you already, hmm a woman who knows how to follow instructions." He replied.

"Whatever man, I see you got jokes. Send me your address and I should be there in about 30-45 minutes."

"I'm sending it now," Jonathan replied.

"Cool, see you soon."

Jonathan can now put his plans into place to see if Stephanie is as obedient as she is stubborn. *Yes, Ms. Xavier in the next 30-45 minutes I will see how submissive you are...see you soon Ms. Xavier.*

Stephanie

Quickly rushing to Kelsey's office, Stephanie needed to speak with her before they both left the office for the evening. Tapping lightly on her door and opening it at the same time, Kelsey was sitting at her desk staring at her cell phone.

"Hey sis, you got a quick second?" I asked as I proceed to walk into her office.

"Sure, what's up?" Kelsey questioned.

"I'm going over to the police officer's house for drinks. I will text you his information when I get there. Police officer or not – hell, crazy is crazy." I giggled.

"Hell yeah, be sure and send me the information, 'cuz crazy knows crazy and between the two of us, we know a lot of these fools out here," Kelsey stated in a matter of fact way.

"I shouldn't be there too long; I will call you when I get home tonight. Love you much, sis."

"Get the hell outta here with that mushy shit." Kelsey laughed. "Love you too, S.E.X."

I felt a little strange leaving out of Kelsey's office, she never calls me S.E.X.

That's weird, well weirder things have happened in my life, so oh well.

Grabbing her phone and keys, Stephanie heads out to Jonathan's house, even though she had a nice weekend with Cedric, she could use some more dick. Technically they are not a couple, so she is not cheating.

Why am I even thinking about sleeping with this guy? Hell, who am I kidding, he is sexy and a bit rugged- of course I am having sex with him – hell, he looks like he fucks, and I could use a good fuck tonight.

Ring… Ring… (Unknown caller)

Here we go with this bullshit, I refused to answer. Ignoring the call, Stephanie plugged Jonathan's address into the GPS. Now, it was time for her to have a good night. She was ready for a nice glass of wine, conversation from a different point of view, and a night to relax and unwind. Pulling up at Jonathan's house made Stephanie inhale a deep breath. He lived in a beautiful two-story house with three garages, in a nice subdivision. She did not know what to expect but this house was breathtaking, the landscaping was well manicured, the front porch had white rocking chairs on them, and the view just made her smile. This was a home, not just a house. She could not wait to get inside to see how well it was decorated. Quickly approaching the front door, she inhaled and exhaled before she rang the doorbell and when Jonathan opened the front door, there was a glimmer in his eyes that almost scared her.

"Hello beautiful," Jonathan said.

"Hi."

"Thanks for coming over." Stepping to the side so Stephanie could enter the house, he mentioned, "Please come in."

"Thank you for inviting me over, you have a beautiful house."

"Aww thanks, just a lil sumthin, sumthin." He chuckled.

"Hmm ok, well I am loving the sumthin, sumthin."

"I will be sure to give you a tour before you leave." He replied.

Gently holding her hand, he guided her to the kitchen area. He reached for a glass of white wine he had previously poured and handed it to her. She smiled as she sipped the wine.

"Mmm this is good, and whatever you are cooking smells delicious."

"I whipped up some shrimp scampi pasta. I figured you would be hungry after a long day at work in the office." He mentioned.

"Well, I am kinda hungry, that was thoughtful. I guess my first impression of you was very wrong."

Wrinkling his forehead, he questioned, "So what was your first impression?"

"I thought you were a true asshole."

Gazing into her eyes he questioned, "And now what do you think?"

Feeling the hairs stand up on the back of her neck as she challenged his gaze, she replied, "You're not too bad after all."

"Well, thank you for a change of heart, Ms. Xavier."

"My pleasure."

After a delicious meal and some entertaining conversation, three hours had passed and neither one of them realized how late it was. It seemed neither wanted the evening to end. As Jonathan reached for their third bottle of wine, Stephanie suddenly realized it was dark outside.

"Oh, my goodness, I lost track of time, I should be heading home."

Touching her hand, Jonathan questioned, "Do you really have to leave?"

Before she could respond, he leaned in and kissed her. The kiss was hot; it ignited a fire within her that she was not aware existed. Not protesting, she embraced his lips and allowed his hands to explore her body. The wetness she felt in between her legs was uncontrollable; without another word, he lifted her arms and descended down the stairs to the basement. Stephanie was so lost in the kiss; she felt as if she was floating - she did not realize he had moved her until he placed her onto a bed. Breaking their kiss, she looked around and was shocked, almost scared of everything she saw. It was a room full of foreign objects (foreign to her) of course she has had her role in the hay and her pleasure with sex toys, but this was on another level - a Fifty Shades of Gray level.

Before she could question anything, Jonathan looked into her eyes and questioned, "Do you trust me?"

Too afraid to speak, I simply nodded my head.

"Good, I have been waiting so long to get you here."

"What?"

"Shhh, just close your eyes and let me please you," he said.

And I did exactly as he said.

"Close your eyes and open your mouth."

I complied.

"I'm going to blindfold you, and I am going to place something in your mouth, you won't be able to speak, but it won't hurt either."

He climbed on the bed and put the blindfold on me and inserted a ball in my mouth and fastened it behind my head. He then unzipped my dress, removed my panties, which were soaked from the anticipation, the mystery, and the sexiness of it all. I am too shocked to move.

"Open your legs and lie back." He commanded. I froze - all kinds of thoughts are racing through my mind, I guess he sensed the hesitation, so he leaned in and kissed me again, and once again I started to relax. His gently pushed me back and his kisses trailed down my body. He went to my wet spot, and like a kitten, he gently licked me, and I squirmed. His licks were soft, but strong and my body heated up, and I reached down to touch him.

"STOP!" He commands "You are only allowed to do what I say. Do you understand?"

Fear caused me to sit straight up on the bed; a million things were running through my mind. He began to insert his fingers into my wetness, and I spread my legs to welcome them. He then inserted a vibrator and I am trying not to cum. The feeling was so intense, then suddenly the vibrator stopped, the room was still, quiet, too quiet, I don't hear Jonathan moving around. I tried to gain a sense of what was going on around me and in a split second, the vibrator started again, and I feel pleasure all over again.

Jonathan continued to play with his remote-control vibrator for a few minutes as he sat in the corner pleasing himself. He enjoyed watching her squirm from the pleasure and the anticipation. Having his fill of playing with her, now it was time to get down to business. He turned the vibrator off and approached the bed where Stephanie laid, but on his way to the bed he grabs his black riding crop and slowly glides it across her body, and she jumps. He teases her with the crop.

Whack...Whack

She cries out in pain.

Whack...Whack

Slowly, the tears start to trickle down her face. He removes the ball from her mouth but leaves the blindfold on her eyes.

"Are you ready for some more?" He whispered.

"No, I can't take anymore." Stephanie panted.

"Say yes." He commanded.

"No, I don't want to play anymore, I am leaving," Stephanie said as she attempted to remove the blindfold.

But, before she could, he suddenly grabbed her hands, "We aren't done yet, there is so much more I want to do to you and with you. Play with me a little while longer." He said as he turned the vibrator on again.

Stephanie falls back on the bed. As much as she wanted this game to end, she was still curious as to what else he had in store for her. Jonathan slowed the level on the vibrator and attached clamps to her nipples which heightened the pain and increased her pleasure; he then rolled her on her stomach and proceeded to lick her asshole. At first Stephanie protested, but as Jonathan continued to lick the more she relaxed and liked it. Her head was spinning, and her pussy was drench from constantly cumming. Stephanie cried, screamed, and begged for more. Jonathan removed her blindfold and kissed her on her forehead.

"Are you ready for more?" He questioned as he gazed in her eyes.

Stephanie refused to answer him. Taking this as a part of the game, he quickly grabbed her by her throat and began to fuck her rough with his fingers.

"I said, are you ready for more?"

"Yes." Stephanie did not even recognize her own voice.

"Yes what?"

"Yes, Jonathan."

"My name is Master. Tell me you are ready and address me as Master." He commanded.

"Yes, Master," Stephanie replied.

"Are you enjoying yourself?"

"Yes, Master."

"Very good, you are a quick learner." He smiled. *She is ready for me. I knew she was going to be worth the wait.*

Releasing his thick eight-inch dick from his pants, he could not wait to be inside of her. His dick slid into her wetness and a jolt of electricity was felt between the both of them. Stephanie wrapped her legs around his waist as he grabbed her ass and began pounding. He could feel her on the verge of climaxing.

"Don't cum until I tell you to." He mentioned as his eyes burned into her flesh.

"I'm about to…."

"DO AS I SAY!"

"I can't wait."

Releasing her ass with one hand, he grabs her by the face and stares at her, almost through her. The passion between them caused Stephanie to close her eyes. She did not want this moment to end.

"Open your eyes and look at me." He commanded.

She complies.

"Tell me you love me."

"What?"

"SAY IT!"

"I love you." She barely whispered.

"Now you can cum."

And she did exactly as he said, and he went down and licked her pussy. He needed and wanted to taste her, and without notice he came on her chest. His cum was hot and thick and without another thought, Stephanie dragged her finger through it, put her fingers in her mouth and savored the moment. In a quick motion, Jonathan moved off of the bed, told her there was a bathroom next door, and told her to let herself out after she cleaned herself off.

"What?" She questioned.

"You heard me, text me so that I know you made it home," he said as he closed the door behind him.

"YOU ARE AN ASSHOLE!" Stephanie screamed as she threw the vibrator at him, but it was too late, it hit the door as Jonathan walked out of the room.

Stephanie was now pissed, mad, embarrassed, and feeling the lowest of the low. What in the fuck was she thinking? In between her tears and her fumbling to find her clothes, she did not even clean him off of her, she went up the stairs and to her car, and drove away... not even looking in her rearview mirror.

Cedric

Cedric has been traveling and putting fires out and saving companies for the last few weeks, but now he is finally back at home and settled. He has checked in with Stephanie periodically, but something has changed between them. The last visit they had was perfect; he could not have asked for anything more. Stephanie did something to him. He was starting to feel things he had not felt in a long time... happiness, peace, and jealousy but he was not ready to accept any of those emotions. Shaking off the thought, he picked up his cell phone and the business card that has been taunting him for the last few days.

"Hello, who is speaking?" The caller asked.

"Walter, this is Cedric. Cedric Armstrong. We met a few weeks ago."

"Well hello Cedric. What do I owe the pleasure?"

"I wanted to finish our conversation from a few weeks ago. Do you have a few minutes?" Cedric questioned as his body tensed with anxiety.

"Absolutely! What seems to be on your mind?" Walter questioned. He did not realize how excited he was to receive this phone call. *What does he really want?* Walter thought.

"When I saw you last, it seemed like you had more to say about my girl... I mean Stephanie, so I wanted to finish our conversation."

Chuckling Walter replied, "Well she has been my neighbor for over 5 years. Our conversations are far and few in between. She is a headstrong woman who doesn't like people meddling in her business - if you catch my drift."

"Oh, trust me I know, but that description could be half of the black women in my office building. Don't bullshit me by wasting my time; I know there is more that you know." Cedric was beginning to get irritated with Walter's useless information.

"Slow down my brother, remember you called me." Walter snapped.

"My apologies, but there has to be more - she drives me insane; I am crazy about this woman and I need to be sure everything is legit with her. Do you see her with other guys? Have you ever heard anything about her past, her ex-husband, her family? Look man, I am desperate to find out any and everything I can about her."

"She is very secretive, very guarded. I tried my hand at attempting to take her out but apparently, I was not her type. For some unknown reason she truly dislikes me, but to answer your questions, she is sexy of course you know that, so of course I have seen cars come and go over the years; however, lately you are the only one I have seen in a while. Little Ms. Stephanie has seemed to have slowed down over the past years." Walters chuckles again.

"Well it seems you are enjoying this conversation a little too much," Cedric mentions.

"Oh, trust me; you have no idea how much. Let me give you some parting words - you're a lucky man, but I am sure you already know that, but sometimes you should just show up and surprise her... Stephanie loves surprises." Chuckling, Walter disconnected the call.

Cedric threw his cell phone across the room; he was frustrated with himself for calling Walter and frustrated with Walter for wasting his time.

Okay Walter, thank you for your little advice...she likes surprises huh...well I will be sure to keep that in mind.

Grabbing his laptop, Cedric decided to do the one thing he should have done from the beginning - an extensive background check on Stephanie. He needed answers and he was going to find out all there was on Ms. Stephanie Xavier, one way or another.

Jonathan

After Stephanie left Jonathan's house, he was floating from the adrenaline... she was everything he envisioned... beautiful, sexy, shy, wet, and oh so tasty. Maybe he could have handled his exit strategy a little better, but he was in the moment and that's how he normally dismissed the others. *But she's not liked the others.*

"I have to see her again," Jonathan whispers to himself. Reaching for his cell phone, he calls her... hmm voicemail. Making an effort to sound joyful Jonathan decided to leave a message. "Hi Stephanie, it's Jonathan, I wanted to give you a call... I have been thinking about you and wanted to see if I could, maybe take you out to the movies this week. Hit me back when you get this message. Later."

Ending the call, Jonathan could feel the heat rising within his body. Speaking to no one in particular, he once again whispers,

"Trust me Stephanie, I will be with you again. I have waited for you... someone like you for a long time. You will be mine."

Deciding to get out of the house for some fresh air, Jonathan punches in Stephanie's address into his GPS. He took a picture of her ID the day he pulled her over. *A quick drive-by won't do any harm. Besides I need to see how and where she lives.*

After driving for about 30 minutes Jonathan pulled into a beautiful subdivision, a very impressive subdivision. He was actually shocked by what he saw. *I guess Ms. Xavier is doing pretty well for herself.* Approaching her house (according to the GPS) Jonathan stopped the car to get a look at her place. Apparently, he was staring too long because a man appears out of nowhere and tapped on his window. *What the fuck?*

"How can I help you?" I ask this stranger as my window went down.

"Umm, I'm the one asking questions," Walter barks.

"What do you want?"

"I want to know what is so fascinating about this house that has you gawking at it," Walter mentioned as he pointed towards Stephanie's house.

Frowning, Jonathan questioned, "Is that your house?"

"It could be. What is it to you, bruh?"

"Bruh? Dude we did not come from the same pussy, I ain't your bruh."

"I was trying to be neighborly, but now I have to be a nigga - how is this mutherfucking house any of your concern?" Walter inquired.

"Yo old man, step away from my car, or I will move you."

"Yep, just like I thought - a straight nigga. Come on boy, do what you got to do." Walter gestures with open arms.

In one swift move, Jonathan pulls his gun out and aims it at Walter. "Now you want to move or be moved?"

Walter quickly steps back as Jonathan sped off, leaving smoke from his wheels. "Fuck you!" Walter yelled.

Jonathan gives him the finger as he turned the corner.

Fucking bastard. Walter thought.

Stephanie

Stepping out of my house, I hear Weirdo Walter yelling in the middle of the street. Proceeding with caution hoping to be invisible to him, I tried to make it to my car before he noticed me, but no such luck.

"Well good day to you, Stephanie."

Shit. "Hi Walter," I say as I try to increase my pace. "What are you ranting about and why are you standing it in the middle of the street?"

"Just working on keeping the neighborhood safe and most importantly making sure you are safe and secure."

"Me?" I point to myself. "You don't have to do anything for me."

"Trust me beautiful; I am always looking out for you," Walter said with a sinister grin.

"Whatever."

"So how is Cedric?"

"What? That's none of your business." I snapped.

"Oh, I could easily make it my business; you know he is just a phone call away."

"Walter, please do me a favor and go stand back in the middle of the street... be sure to stand in line with my car so I can run your short ass over."

"Owww testy, aren't we? Maybe I need to come over tonight and run my dick in and out of your delicious pussy." Walter mentions, practically drooling at the thought.

"Go fuck yourself you pervert, and if I ever catch you on my property again, trust me you will get more than an eyeful of me fucking someone, I will taze your nasty ass," I yell as I slammed my car door.

"Well, just know the offer stands when you're ready." Walter chuckled.

I wish he would die.

Kelsey

Kelsey has been home recovering - too embarrassed to talk to anyone; she has never felt so alone in her life. Since it was Sunday, she decided to skip church and sleep in and enjoy the quiet time. She noticed several missed calls from DaShawn but heck he is one phone call away from being blocked. Ever since some mysterious flowers arrived at her house, she felt she could not trust anyone, and everyone was a suspect.

(3 days before)

"Kelsey, who sent you flowers?" Barry inquired.

"Flowers? What did the card say?"

"If there was a card, do you think I would be asking the damn question?"

"Whoa partner, who in da hell are you talking to?" Kelsey asked as she closed the space between the two of them.

"Kelsey, I have put up with enough of your shit over the last couple of months. You are two seconds away from getting your ass tossed on the front porch."

"Barry, consider this your warning, I'm not about to be disrespected from your corny ass. You got me fucked up with one of your friends."

"Kiss my ass, Kelsey." Barry snorted.

"I'm about to bust your ass if you keep running your mou..."

Before she could finish her statement, the vase and flowers came flying across the room. Barry had turned into a mad man. Years of anger and frustration overtook him; before he could gain control, he lunged at Kelsey and grabbed her by her throat... all he saw was red. He was foaming at the mouth and calling Kelsey by every name in the book. The next thing he remembered was seeing stars. Kelsey had managed to grab a picture hanging on the wall and smashed it across his head. Kelsey did not know who this man was standing before her bleeding from the cut on his forehead, but as crazy as it may sound, she had a newfound respect for Barry. Barry finally felt like the man of the house - he walked away leaving her on the floor gasping for air. He smirked to himself but also winced from the pain on his forehead. He knew he was wrong for hurting her but in his mind, he knew she deserved it and besides the damage has been done.

(Present day)

Kelsey still had the bruises on her neck, but she refused to bring the situation up again with Barry or anyone else for that matter. Barry did not seem to care because he has not spoken to her since the fight. He didn't even wake her up for church that morning.

Oh well, now I see how he is and how I have to be, Kelsey thought to herself.

Ring

"Yes." No need for pleasantries, he is calling my damn phone.

"I'm on my way home and I have company with me so be presentable," Barry demanded.

"Who is…"

Click

"Oh, now this bitch is tripping. I am going to embarrass his ass as soon as he walks in this house. I don't give a fuck who is with him. Lord Jesus, this bitch got me cursing on Your day… please forgive me... shit." Kelsey said out loud.

Twenty minutes later Barry walked in the house laughing and talking to someone. Kelsey walked out of the room and almost passed out…it was DaShawn standing in her house with her husband."

"DaShawn I would like for you to meet my wife Kelsey," Barry said as he walked over to embrace Kelsey.

Sweet Jesus. Kelsey thought.

"Well, aren't you beautiful, it's nice to meet you Keisha."

"Kelsey." She corrected him while throwing daggers with her eyes.

"Oh, I'm sorry Kelsey, please forgive me." DaShawn smiles. "You look familiar, have we met before?"

"Naw man, but I get that a lot." Kelsey looks at the both of them and questioned, "How do you two know each other?"

"It's a crazy story, but I will fill you in after I run to the restroom. Make yourself comfortable and I will be right back. Kelsey why don't you fix our guest a drink... act like you have some manners." Barry mentioned as he gives Kelsey a little shove, as he exits the living room.

"What in the fuck are you doing in my house?" Kelsey said as she clenched her teeth.

"Well, if the mountain won't come to Mohammed then..."

"Do you know I will slice your throat right here on my white sofa?" Kelsey questioned.

"What's wrong honey? You seem a bit upset." DaShawn chuckled.

"Is this funny to you? How do you even know my husband?"

"Oh, Barry will tell you the story, it's such a small world. By the way, did you like the flowers?"

"You punk ass bitch, you sent those flowers? What did I do to you? All of a sudden you have your pink panties in a bunch?" Kelsey spat.

"You did nothing sweetness, and that was the problem. Remember, nobody puts Baby in the corner. I saw you at the bar with the white dude, since when did you like white meat? And besides, I was tired of you ignoring my calls. I had to show you who was the boss in this relationship."

"Relationship? You know what, I am trying not to cuss on the Lord's Day, but fuck it, you deserve every word coming out of my mouth."

"So, I see the two of you are getting acquainted," Barry said, as he re-entered the room. "So, did DaShawn mention how we know each other?"

"Actually, I was just about to tell my sister-in-law the news," DaShawn claimed.

"Sister-in-law?" What in the fuck are you talking about?" Kelsey practically screamed.

"DaShawn is my half-brother. He approached me after church today, and we started chatting just to find out we knew a few of the same people, and who would have thought that we are actually related." Barry beamed. "It was such a coincidence, but I think I do remember being around him when I was a kid, but that was so long ago. I cannot believe this is happening."

"You can say that shit again," Kelsey replied.

"Well, I am so happy we are together again. We have so much to talk about and share. I like sharing." DaShawn mentioned with a sinister grin.

"You mentioned something about staying at a shelter because you lost your house, well as your big brother I can't have you staying at a shelter, we have plenty of room here, so maybe you should think about staying here for a while. Kelsey..."

Before Barry could finish his statement, Kelsey fainted.

Justin

Justin had managed to obtain half of the money he needed so the private investigator could provide the rest of the information he wanted. A few days ago, he met with this mental health counselor (only because it was court-ordered) and mentioned to him that he had a lead on finding Stephanie. His counselor did not think that was a good idea, but Justin knew what was best for him, and no one was going to tell him otherwise. Enjoying the warm weather, Justin decided to venture downtown so he could think of other ways to come up with the rest of the money he needed. He suddenly heard some music coming from a bar called The Red Rooster, he chuckled to himself thinking what a stupid name for a bar, but heck the music was jumping.

"Hi, welcome to The Red Rooster. Would you like a table, or do you prefer to sit at the bar?" The hostess greeted him.

"I will take a table please."

"How many people will be joining you?"

"It's just me," Justin replied.

"Well, you're a handsome man, so I'm sure you won't be alone for long."

Laughing, Justin replied, "That's what's up." Justin followed the hostess to a table that gave a view of the entire bar, which was perfect for him. This would allow him to see who he could pick up for the night... he needed the rest of the money by any means necessary.

"Someone will be with you shortly to take your order." The hostess mentioned as she handed him a menu.

"Cool."

As Justin examined the menu, and took in the scenery, his mind and body started to relax and calm down. *This might not have been a bad idea, after all,* he thought to himself. As he reviewed the menu, it suddenly occurred to him that he was tapping his feet and humming along to the music the band was playing.

"Hi, my name is Alacia, I will be your server tonight. Can I get you started with a drink or maybe an appetizer?"

"Everything looks good, but for now I will start with an order of hot wings, and a Seagram's 7, straight."

"Okay, I will put your order in right away." Alacia smiled and walked away.

Justin is enjoying the music and the atmosphere, all of the women are absolutely beautiful, everyone had his attention, but this one lady, in particular had ALL of his attention.

"It can't be. It's not possible." Justin whispers to himself. As if he was in a trance, he slid out of his chair and walked across the bar and stopped at her table.

"Hello," Justin says.

Not looking up from her phone, she replied, "I'm not interested."

"Excuse me?"

"Umm again, I am not interested, please leave me alone." She replied, still dismissing him.

"But umm..."

"Dude, I was trying to be nice, but apparently you cannot take a hint. What part of go away do you not understand?"

"STEPHANIE!" Justin yelled.

Dropping her phone, Stephanie froze.

Stephanie

I'm sitting in The Red Rooster, waiting on Cedric, when I receive a text from him saying his flight was canceled. Now I am upset and pissed and this dude had the nerve to approach my table trying to have a conversation that I am not up to having, so I tried my best to dismiss him but he clearly cannot take a hint, and then suddenly he called my name. And in a quick second, I am staring in the eyes of the devil. This can't be possible, I actually thought he was dead, hell I prayed every day that he died a slow painful death.

"What do you want? How did you even find me?" I questioned, trying to sound brave, but my body was full of terror.

"I want you; I have been searching for you ever since you left," Justin replied with excitement in his voice.

Wrinkling my eyebrows, I responded, "Well, I won't even tell that lie to you and say the feeling is mutual because it is not. Well, now that you have seen me, you can check that off of your list, and walk away." I mentioned as I shooed him away. Not liking the dismissive attitude and the disrespect he is received from Stephanie; he suddenly changed his disposition. "Who in the fuck do you think you're talking to?" Justin yelled once again. *Now this is the Justin I remember.* "I'm not the Stephanie I used to be, so I suggest you leave me alone." Fear is all over my body, but it doesn't come across in my voice. "Go away!" "I'm not leaving until you agree to hear me out. Let me explain myself." Justin said as he tried to slide in the booth. As he came in on one side, I am sliding out of the booth on the other side, but he is quicker than I am, he grabbed my arm and the memories of my past begin to return. Once again, I froze. "Is everything okay over here?" Jonathan questioned. I swear I have never been more excited to see anyone before in my entire life.

"Sure, everything is good over here," Justin replied.

"Stephanie is everything okay?" Jonathan questioned.

Squeezing my arm tighter, Justin said "Babe tell him everything is okay."

"I was talking to the lady," Jonathan mentioned never taking his eyes off of me.

"Look punk, you don't want none of this. I am having a conversation with my wife. In fact, how do you even know her?" Justin questioned as he released my arm and proceeded to slide out of the booth.

Standing toe to toe, eye to eye, these two are about to set it off in this place, and I am attempting to exit stage right.

Jonathan lifted his shirt ever so slightly to reveal his gun and badge and replied, "It's none of your business how I know her, but from the looks of things, she doesn't want to be bothered. So, I suggest you leave her alone."

Looking down Justin noticed his badge and gun, takes a step back and glared at me, "This is not over Stephanie, we will finish this conversation."

I heard him say as I headed towards the exit, Jonathan is following me and calling my name, but I did not look back until I was outside of the bar, then I finally took a breath. Jonathan stopped me in mid-step.

"Thank you for saving me."

"My pleasure, are you okay? Jonathan asked.

"I'm okay now."

"What was that all about? You're married?"

"Hell no! That is my ex-husband." Pausing for a second, I suddenly realize Jonathan is standing in front of me.

"What are you doing here?"

Smiling he replied, "This is my spot. I'm always in here."

"No way, I have never seen you in here."

"Well I have seen you here before, in fact, where is the other lady you're always with?" Jonathan questioned.

"Umm okay, that's a bit creepy," I mentioned, half-joking, half-serious. "She didn't come into the office today. I was supposed to meet a friend here, but his flight got canceled so I'm going home."

"Oh, a dude huh?"

"Don't even go there Jonathan. YOU and I need to have a conversation about that little stunt you pulled the other night, but unfortunately it will not be tonight. I will give you a call later, but seriously, thank you for rescuing me." I replied as I leaned in for a hug.

"I look forward to the conversation," Justin whispered in my ear. Before he released me, he kissed me on my cheek. "Text me so I know you made it home safe."

"Will do."

"Promise?"

"Yes, I promise."

Stephanie rushed to her car, not even realizing she is being watched.

Kelsey

"*This clearly is a bad dream*", Kelsey thought to herself. A week ago, Barry had the nerve to make the decision to invite DaShawn to move in with them. Ever since the two of them have reunited, they have been inseparable with the constant hanging out, catching up from lost time and all the crazy shit "boys do" ... hanging out, staying up late talking, and bonding over old and pointless shit. Kelsey has felt ignored, deflated, rejected, and overall miserable. She had to figure out how to get control of her life once again. Her mind drifted to Stephanie; Kelsey has not been a friend to anyone lately but to totally shut Stephanie out was something Kelsey did not think she would have ever done... *"It's time to bring the BITCH back...once again...GAME ON!"*

Kelsey had to bounce back from the foolishness around her, so she decided to get her sexy on; walking to the closet in her bedroom, she found a dress that captures all of her curves, plugged in her flat iron, she turned on some Ledisi, and retreated to the shower. Kelsey stepped out of the shower feeling refreshed, not only was she going to look beautiful, she was going to put all of her effort into feeling beautiful... now if she could continue to maintain that confidence once she steps outside of her bedroom. Gliding down the hallway as if she was moving in slow motion, she ascended to the kitchen, just to find out the entire house was empty. *Good, these mutherfuckers aren't even home.* Pouring herself a glass of wine, (even though it was only 11:00 a.m.in the morning), she felt like she needed a tall glass at that very moment. She poured wine to the brim of here glass, grabbed the bottle, and her cell phone and moved to her favorite chair in her den. She decided to finally check all of her voicemail messages. As she reclined on the lounge chair in the family room, she listened to messages from Scott, Stephanie, and some irrelevant messages from DaShawn. "Oh well, I will return calls later today,"

Kelsey mentioned as she poured herself another glass.

Thirty minutes later, Kelsey seemingly dozed off - partly because she was exhausted but mainly because she was tipsy. Feeling kisses on her neck, she was not sure if she was in a dream, but the kisses did feel good, so she welcomed the attention. Slowly returning the act, she was getting aroused, moist, and turned on.

"Tell me you miss me." He said.

Suddenly opening her eyes, Kelsey found DaShawn on her... kissing and touching her. It took every muscle in her body to attempt to push DaShawn off of her.

"Have you lost your damn mind?" Kelsey screamed.

"Don't act like you don't want me. I mean look at you, lookin' all sexy 'n stuff. Don't resist, think about the old times. I can make you feel good." DaShawn pleaded with her.

"If you don't get the fuck off of me, you are going to regret ever stepping foot into my house. I'm not Barry, I will fuck you up." Kelsey mentioned as she attempted to stand up.

DaShawn was quicker than she was; he lunged at her, causing her to fall back on the chair. He tried to rip her clothes off. DaShawn was determined to make Kelsey pay for disrespecting him these past few months. He slapped her, then his hands found her neck and he began choking her. Has was too strong for Kelsey, but she still tried to scratch and hit him. In the midst of DaShawn drawing his fist back to punch Kelsey in the face, Barry tackled him, and all three of them landed on the floor. Kelsey is gasping for air; she knew she needed to do something to stop this fight. As she struggled to her feet, Kelsey felt anger, so she decided to join in the fight, and began kicking DaShawn, but being the petty person, she is, she got in a few kicks to Barry's ass as well. *(that's for putting me in the middle of this shit!)*

DaShawn was no match for Barry. "What in the fuck is going on?" Barry questioned DaShawn as he straddled him.

"Fuck you!" DaShawn pants in between breathes.

"Fuck me? You better answer me, or I will fuck you up." Barry screamed.

"Barry!" Kelsey cried out.

"Go ahead sister-in-law; tell your husband what's going on."

"SHUT-UP!" Kelsey screams as she kicks DaShawn in his ribs.

"Bitch!" DaShawn winced in pain.

"Kelsey, go get my gun," Barry commanded.

Kelsey flees to the bedroom to retrieve Barry's gun, returning to the den, she points the gun at DaShawn.

"I am about to release you, but if you make one wrong move, I give my wife permission to put a bullet in your head."

"And you know I will!" Kelsey responded.

As Barry moved, DaShawn slowly crawled to a standing position.

"Now what in the hell is going on in my house?" Looking between the two of them, Barry demanded an answer.

"This punk-ass attacked me," Kelsey yelled.

"You begged me to have sex with you." DaShawn lied.

"Babe let me shoot him," Kelsey begged as she waved the gun in his face.

"Calm down." Barry raised his hands to stop Kelsey.

"Tell him Kelsey. Tell him who I am to you. Tell him or I WILL." DaShawn yelled.

Smack! Kelsey slapped him across his face.

Laughing in a sinister voice, DaShawn yelled, "TELL HIM."

"Kelsey, what is he talking about?" Barry inquired.

"Nothing, I have no clue what the fuck he is rambling about."

"Enough of the bullshit, I'm calling my boys, it's time for you leave," Barry announced. As he picked up his cell phone to make a call; he is giving commands to whoever is on the other end. Kelsey glared at DaShawn, regretting ever giving him the time of day.

"Your world is about to change, Ms. Lady." DaShawn

chuckled.

"You're talking to me as if you don't see this gun in my hand."

"As soon as he gets done with his call, I'm singing like a ..."

"Like the bitch that you are?" Kelsey interrupts DaShawn.

Before the conversation could continue, two uniformed police officers walked into the den, handcuffs presented, and guns drawn.

"Take his sorry ass out of here," Barry demanded.

"What the fuck?" DaShawn questioned. "Barry, you're my brother, what is happening?"

"You tried to rape my wife."

"RAPE?"

"You have the right to remain silent." One of the officers mentioned.

"Hold up - this is some bullshit. Kelsey wanted me. Tell him, Kelsey. Tell your husband how we have been fucking for the last few months. TELL HIM!" DaShawn demanded. "Room 215 at the Crowne Plaza." DaShawn tussles with the officers in the midst of his outbursts. "TELL HIM!"

Finally tuning in to DaShawn's rants, Barry stopped the officer and questioned, "What are you talking about?"

"Babe, he is crazy, don't listen to him." Kelsey attempted to pull Barry away from DaShawn.

"Don't touch me." Barry snapped at Kelsey and redirected his attention back to DaShawn. "What are you talking about?"

"I'm talking about me and your wife - have been fucking for the last few months. Unnhuh, I have had her every which way possible, and trust me, big brother, the pussy is delicious. Now, I see why you let her treat you like crap; it is because her pussy got that monkey - it makes you wanna smack ya...."

Before DaShawn could finish, Barry punched him in his face.

"Get this bitch out of my house. I will be at the station in a few minutes to complete the paperwork."

As the officers hauled kicking and screaming DaShawn out of the house, Kelsey stood frozen waiting on Barry to make eye contact with her and once he did, he said, "Pack your shit and get the hell out of my house."

"Barry wait!" Kelsey cried out.

But it was too late; Barry slammed the front door as he left the house.

Cedric

The next day, Cedric was finally able to get a flight, but he chose not to tell Stephanie of his pending arrival. He was taking Walter up on his suggestion of surprising her, maybe if he popped up, he would finally get the answer to a lot of the unanswered questions he needed - more like wanted answers. He tried calling and texting her last night, but he guesses she was upset because his flight was canceled. There are some things in life that you have no control over. He felt like he was totally invested in her and the last thing he wanted to do was disappoint her, but things happen in life.

Stepping off of the plane and finding his assigned Uber, Cedric made one final attempt to call Stephanie but again, no such luck. He then calls her office; however, the secretary mentioned she has yet to arrive. Disconnecting the call, he silently told himself to not over-think things; she just overslept or at least that's the explanation that is keeping him calm.

Reaching her house, he noticed several cars in her driveway. As he stepped out of the car, another guy pulls up as well. *What in the hell is going on?*

The two men, size each other up. "Hey, can I help you?" Cedric questioned.

"I am just checking on my friend's house. I received a strange phone call and I just want to make sure everything is okay." Jonathan spoke with caution.

"Your friend? Are you sure you're at the right house?" Cedric questioned with a puzzled look on his face.

"I am positive, and who are you?"

"I guess I'm a friend of the homeowner, as well. It seemed like she has a lot of friends."

"Well, I would suggest you stay out here until I go make sure everything is okay." Jonathan proposed.

"Stay in your lane, I'm no punk, you walk… I walk."

"Look, man, I don't have time to debate with you, I need to…."

BOOM

Immediately, Cedric and Jonathan take off running towards Stephanie's house.

Stephanie

(Present day)

"You Bitch! I'm going to kill you!" She screamed.

She grabbed me by my hair, and we both fall to the floor. During the struggle, I get the upper hand… so I thought.

"Slaaaap!"

The strange woman slapped me so hard, I momentarily blacked out. When I regained consciousness, I saw double. There she is with a gun in my face.

"What do you have to say for yourself, hoe?"

I asked her, "Who are you? What do you want? Why are you here?"

I have no clue who she is, how she got in my house, and more importantly, what in the hell does she want.

She waves the gun at me as she screamed on the phone to someone.

"How could you let this happen? What did I do wrong? What do you see in this bitch?"

Now, I'm pissed! I feel blood drip down from my face; my $300 Donna Karan dress is now worth about $3.00 and this deranged bitch has the nerve to be upset... really? Who does this?

She hangs up the phone and focused her attention back to me, then asked the million-dollar question. "Why are you fucking my man?"

The question I am asking myself is...*Who in the hell is her man?*

Feeling overly confident, I decided to ask the million-dollar question, "Who in the fuck is your man?"

"Don't act as if you don't know. I have seen the both of you together several times. Do you think I'm stupid?"

"If you weren't holding a gun in my face, I would really answer that question," I replied as I wiped the dripping blood from my lip.

The mystery woman is pacing back and forth and making me very nervous, but I really think I can get the gun from her and once I do, I am going to whip her ass. My brain is on speed trying to figure out who this chick is and why is she bothering me. I mean, let's be serious, I have not been a saint when it comes to men, bottom line is, hell if they want me, then all bets are off. As this fool is still yelling to whomever on the phone, she turns her back to me, and now I see my opportunity to lunge at her. As I grabbed her from behind, I did not realize how strong this bitch really was, but we are going to fight to the end…one of us is going to die today.

BOOM

The gun goes off and we both are now staring at one another, I am not sure what is happening, but this bitch is screaming, and when I look down, I see blood seeping through my dress… I am getting weak, I suddenly fall to the floor, my breathing is slow, and a rush of thoughts and emotions flooded my mind…everything is moving in slow motion.

As the room goes dark and the coldness in Stephanie's body starts to set in, a single tear rolled down her cheek. One single tear that represented her life, her past, and the twins she lost, her mother, her unknown father, and all of the wives she has disrespected over the years. And in one last breath,

Stephanie closed her eyes and took her last breath

EPILOGUE

It has been two months since the tragic day that Stephanie does not ever want to relive ever again in her life. Cedric and Kelsey have not left her side since the incident. Kelsey and Barry are in a very bad place right now, so the only friend she has is Stephanie. DaShawn was arrested and since he was on probation, he has to complete the remainder of his sentence in jail. It turned out that the mystery woman was Jonathan's ex-fiancé; she had discovered he was still keeping tabs on Stephanie and when she questioned him about who she was, he abruptly ended the relationship.

(June 1992)

Jonathan was a rookie in the police department when he received a call to handle a domestically violent situation. Never having to handle this type of call, he was not sure what to expect. Walking into the apartment, he could see signs of a struggle, but he was not sure who the victim was until he reached the master bedroom and saw a female hovering in the corner. Her back was turned to him, and he could see she was shivering and scared. He immediately took off his jacket and placed it over her shoulders. The act of him doing this made her body relaxed a little. He saw a young frail woman with the saddest eyes. But even behind all her sadness, he saw a beautiful person. He made an attempt to help her up so she could find some clothes (that wasn't torn), she never looked him in his eyes, but she quietly whispered thank you. That simple whisper did something to Jonathan's entire body. He tried to touch her but before he could, a fight broke out in the other room and he had to run out to assist his partner. As he approached the living room, he noticed other officers had arrived so one of the female officers went back to the bedroom to tend to the female victim. At the end of the night, the husband was hauled off to jail and the wife was sent to the hospital for testing. As she was being ushered into the back of the ambulance, he was able to retrieve his jacket from her. His jacket smelled of lavender and lilac, a smell he would never forget. He knew he had to keep up with this female; he had to make her his, and his goal was to always make sure she was safe. He was in love with Stephanie Elizabeth Xavier (S.E.X.).

ACKNOWLEDGMENTS

Man, oh man, where do I start with my acknowledgments. I must give thanks to God, the creator of all things, including ME!! This book has been in the making for over 10 years, and as I sat here and typed the very last letter, my emotions took over. Thank you all for taking the time out of your life to read my book. I hope reading it helped to create the shocking moments, the funny moments, and the hot and steamy moments, I wanted to share with you. As we know, domestic violence is real, and I would never ever take a situation like that lightly. I have been a victim of sexual abuse, verbal abuse, and physical abuse and just like I got out and regained control of my life, I want everyone to know... there is a way out!

This book has been a dream of mine for many, many, many years and I am glad that I had family, and friends who pushed me to continue writing. And to anyone holding this book, I want to thank you for purchasing my book (hopefully you purchased it), please be sure to share your thoughts about it with your friends... don't share your book - have them purchase their own, lol!

Thank you so much for your support.

-Dr. TW

About the Author

Dr. Tracy Washington

Mother, daughter, sister, grandmother, and friend are words used to describe Tracy. Originally from Charleston, South Carolina, Tracy is a graduate of Walden University where she obtained her Doctorate in Business Administration with a concentration in Finance. Currently employed as a full-time Assistant Professor at a university in Knoxville, Tennessee, she teaches finance and business courses on the graduate level. She is also a Court Appointed Special Advocate (CASA) and Guardian Ad Litem (GAL) advocate for Knox County where she works on behalf of children who have experienced abuse or neglect.

Being an educator, an author, a dedicated volunteer, and a motivational speaker allows her the opportunity to do the things that are dear to her heart (helping others). In her spare time, she enjoys cooking, reading, traveling, spending time with her family and sorors. Tracy is a mother to three adult children (Jesse, Antonio, and Kendra) and a grandmother to a beautiful baby girl, (Brielle).

Made in the USA
Columbia, SC
08 July 2020

12714434R00117